AQUARIUS

EDITED BY AUSTIN P. SHEEHAN,
MIKHAEYLA KOPIEVSKY & ALANAH ANDREWS

THE ZODIAC SERIES

The Zodiac Series is a collection of twelve speculative fiction anthologies, each focusing on one of the Zodiac signs. The anthologies feature short stories and poems inspired by each sign, and retellings of the various myths behind those signs.

Capricorn Aquarius Pisces
Aries Taurus Gemini
Cancer Leo Virgo
Libra Scorpio Sagittarius

The Zodiac Series has been produced by Aussie Speculative Fiction, and each anthology contains a diverse selection of tales by talented writers from Australia and New Zealand.

I AM AQUARIUS

Zoey Xolton

I am the Water-Bearer and my constellation is Aquarius.

My tarot card is The Star; I am a champion of the people and a catalyst of change.

At my best I am altruistic, philanthropic and progressive.

At my worst I am unpredictable, stubborn and uncompromising.

Intellectual and free, like my element: Air, mine is a Fixed sign.

I appreciate friends, fun, academic conversation and problem solving.

I dislike boredom, limitations and broken promises.

I am ruled by Uranus, and am guardian to the sixth day of the week.

My colours are blue and silver.

About the Author:

Zoey Xolton is an Australian Speculative Fiction writer, primarily of Dark Fantasy, Paranormal Romance, and Horror. Her works have appeared in over one-hundred themed anthologies, with more due for publication!

She has recently celebrated the release of her debut short story collection Darkly Ever After. *You can find further details regarding her many publications on her website: www.zoeyxolton.com!*

CONTENTS:

I am Aquarius by Zoey Xolton v

Foreword by Sasha Hanton 1

A Pitcher of Water at the End of Days by Pamela Jeffs . 5

She Walks on Frosted Fields by Aiki Flinthart 13

Trident's Song by Nikky Lee 27

The Lighthouse Keeper by Stephen Herczeg 71

Olympus9 by Tee Linden 79

Where Are Your Sheep? by Frank Prem 87

Skewed Futures by Fallacious Rose 91

Brain Trust by Dorian Morrow 101

Monday's Horrorscope by Austin P. Sheehan 127

Dugong Dreaming by Shel Calopa 133

Chain Reaction by Sam M. Phillips 147

Aquaria by Shay Laurent 151

Waterborne by DL Fleming 169

The Water Bearer by Dee Cheers 189

This is the Dawning (Part II) by Helena McAuley 201

FOREWORD

Sasha Hanton

Aquarius, the eleventh sign of the Zodiac, is often mistaken for a water sign but is in fact the last of the air signs. Containing the Latin word 'Aqua' which translates to 'Water' and represented by a water bearer it is no wonder the fixed air sign is commonly confused for a water sign. One of the three Zodiac signs that are ruled by two planets, Aquarius is watched over by Uranus and Saturn.

A variety of myths are associated with the sign of Aquarius across various cultures, though many share similarities and themes. In Egypt, the constellation was associated with Hapi, God of the Nile, who worked to create the rainy season and overflow the Nile River's banks, allowing the waters to nourish the valley farmlands. Many other cultures also associated the water bearer with rainfall or flooding. In Babylon, it was connected to the heavy rains which would fall in their eleventh month causing that time to be referred to as 'the curse of rain'.

In both Greek and Sumerian mythology, Aquarius is associated with a global flood—not unlike the story of Noah and his ark in the Bible—though the myths differ greatly outside of their mention of a global flood. The Sumerian story represents Aquarius as a youth who allowed the floodwaters to flow from the heavens onto the Earth. In the Greek myth, Aquarius represents a couple who survived the flood, Deucalion and Pyrrah, as well as the God who both takes all life from the world and gives it back.

One other myth of Aquarius, which has both a Greek and Roman version, is the tale of Ganymede. This particular myth has multiple interpretations but the core details are that Zeus has an eagle—there is some debate over if this eagle is Zeus himself transformed, a regular eagle, or Zeus' pet giant eagle Aquila (the constellation of Aquila borders Aquarius)—abduct a boy called Ganymede and bring him to the peak of Mount Olympus. Zeus goes on to make Ganymede cupbearer, entrusting him with filling the cups of the Gods with ambrosia, wine, or water whenever they run empty. From there the myth can vary depending on the telling, but the result is always the same with Ganymede sending rains down to earth and Zeus placing him amongst the stars as the constellation Aquarius.

Connections to the Major Arcana of the Tarot are common amongst the Zodiac and this constellation rightfully shares a bond with the 17th card of the Major Arcana, the Star. Most often depicted as a young, naked woman pouring water from two vessels with a large eight-pointed star and seven smaller eight-pointed stars in the sky, it is easy to see the connection between this card and the water-bearer constellation. The woman shown in the Star has one foot placed in the water and one on land, showing a duality in nature, which speaks for Aquarius' split representation between air and water.

The Star is a card symbolic of hope, truth and nourishing the soul (amongst other interpretations), which is fitting as Aquarius individuals are often depicted optimistically and called the humanitarians of the Zodiac. Aquarians stand-out and are often remarked as being aliens for their nature of not blending in. This can be seen in the large central star that dominates the background imagery of the 7th card of the Major Arcana.

With two planets ruling over them, Aquarius natives can lean one way or the other on decisions and perspectives. Saturn, originally the ruling planet for both Capricorn and Aquarius, is strongly associated with time and responsibility, taking its name from the Roman God of time, wealth and agriculture. When Uranus was discovered in 1781 it replaced Saturn as Aquarius' ruling planet. Named for the Greek God, who was also known as Father of the Sky and the Father of the Titans, the discovery of Uranus coincided with the French Revolution and thus the planet became associated with rebellion and lofty ideals.

For those born between January 20th and February 18th, Aquarius is their Sun Sign. Aquarius individuals, with leanings towards Saturn, may be goal-oriented and pragmatic in their approach, coming off as cynical. Those more drawn to Uranus will be highly individualistic, with a zest for freedom and spontaneous conversations.

There is a great duality to Aquarius and as you read through this anthology you are sure to discover even more about this fascinatingly hard-to-pin-down sign.

About the Author:

Sasha Hanton grew up in the tropics of Darwin, Northern Territory. From a young age, she devoured books and iced coffee, both of which she continues to intake on an almost daily basis. Now living on beautiful Bribie Island in Queensland, her time is split between writing and spoiling her puppy Miley.

Sasha, who has a Bachelor of Journalism from Bond University, has dabbled in the journalistic profession but finds fiction far more fascinating. Her first published work The Short Story Press Collection *draws on her love for a diverse range of genres and passion for short stories. Coming from a multicultural background (Eurasian) she aspires to make her writing inclusive for people from all walks of life and to bring a unique blend of eastern and western culture to her writing.*

When she's not writing or reading she can be found walking her dog and volunteering. You can keep up with her writing over on www.theshortstorypress.wordpress.com

A Pitcher of Water at the End of Days

Pamela Jeffs

"Aquarius?"

The name my mother gave me in the hope that I would adopt the traits of the sun sign concludes too much. I am no airy-minded dreamer. I am a space explorer. And one focused on fighting to survive.

"Aquarius?" My husband, Aeon, calls out again. His voice cracks, throat thick with the red dust that gathers in the air. I glance up from the blanket panels I am joining and out the shuttle's port window. My fingers still work the metal needles as I watch the blood-dark dust storm crouching on the horizon.

"In the control room," I reply.

Aeon's boots thud up the metal ladder. Muscled and barrel-chested, he squeezes into the cockpit. He is too large for the small space and his body knows it. I can tell in the way he holds his shoulders hunched forward.

He looks weary, only half the man he was when he flew us out from Space Dock 10. His cheeks are heavy with lines and his bright blue eyes are dulled to grey. Even his uniform looks tired, holes and oil stains marring the knees. "You got that blanket ready?"

I knot the last thread and snip it with the pliers from the console. "Yeah. Ready."

"Good." He dips his head to look out the window and rubs his dusty knuckles under his nose. I notice blood on his wrist, the place where perhaps a wrench tore a hole as he fixed the sub-thrusters. Watching the approaching dust storm, he nods. "It'll be here soon. Better go cover the condensers."

I lay my weaving needles aside and fold the blanket into quarters. "On it," I say.

The air outside smells like petroleum, bitter and burning on the back of my tongue. I swallow, trying to remove the taste but it sticks there. I clutch the blanket to my chest as I head along the side of the craft. Its giant silver hull towers over me like a metal cliff. Scrapes mar the bright steel, scars earned in our forced landing three days ago. Most of the damage is to the rear of the ship. As I approach it, I see Aeon has been busy. The sub-thruster plates are back in place, meaning the focusing crystal cradles have already been re-aligned.

I move past the plates and on to the condensers. Work is ongoing here. The medium sized units, with their shallow funnels and wide turbines, are exposed from behind broken hatches. Usually used to convert ice molecules from interstellar dust into fuel, the components now collect and process water from sand particles. Both units are covered in a thick layer of dust. Too much dust. Not ideal for the working mechanisms and as our only source of water, all the more reason to get them covered before the storm hits.

The breeze kicks up as I approach the units. The storm moves closer. Shards of lightning skitter and circle the dense mass of dark air hanging low in the distance. I turn my face away from the stinging grains of sand carried on the wind. Grit crunches between my teeth. There is a bad feeling to this storm. Uneasy, I unfold the ion blanket I pieced together from four separate sheets. The interwoven metal links clink as I tuck the edges into place around the condensers. I reach into my vest and grab my pocket welder. A green light flicks on when I activate it. The glowing tip makes short work of fusing the blanket to the hull.

I look up and notice the quality of the light has changed. The bright daylight from the planet's three suns has dimmed to dark orange. With the suns obscured behind the approaching dust cloud, the landscape is suddenly far more ominous.

Aeon waits at the gangplank. His broad hand reaches down for me. The wind grows wilder, snapping at my hair. "Hurry up!" he says. "We need to secure the hatch."

I start to run.

I almost reach his hand.

But the dust beats me.

With a sudden drop in atmospheric pressure, the storm is on us. I am flung from the gangway and tossed against the ship's landing strut. Pain lances along my ribcage but soon fades. I look for Aeon. He is still on the gangplank. In shock, I watch him turn and stumble back into the cargo bay. The shuttle door grinds shut. *Is he leaving me out here to die?* All I can do is clutch at my anchor.

I never thought Aeon to be a coward.

My thoughts circle. Perhaps he only left Earth for the glory, to find evidence of alien species to further his own career. Maybe it was never about us taming the universe together. Maybe I was just a contingency plan—something to sacrifice if it was needed.

My anger sits like a rock in my belly.

And the wind is just as angry. It roars around me, twisting and turning like the currents of Earth's far oceans. Waves of sand buffet against me. I squeeze my eyes shut against the stinging onslaught, but the backs of my hands, cheeks and neck suffer the brunt of its vicious touch.

I sob.

Damn Aeon. Damn him to hell. I'm going to die out here.

I force my eyes open to a blurred view of lightning lashing against the dark sky. It is almost beautiful, the way the edges of the electricity skitter and are shattered by the errant winds. Squinting, I look to the ship. Panels are peeling off the hull like scales torn from a fish. I watch them twist up into the sky, before they are thrown away like ruined toys.

A shriek of metal. I glance back at the gangway. The door to the ship opens and Aeon, dressed in his space suit, emerges. My heart leaps. He hasn't abandoned me.

His steps are laboured as his huge bulk presses against the force of the storm. I sob again, guilty for doubting him. He is carrying something. Metal winks in his gloved hand. Another ion blanket.

My desperation turns to hope. If he can get the blanket to me, I can make it to the ship. I close my eyes, huddle my chin to my chest and with hair whipping around my head like serpents, I wait for Aeon.

His hand is like a vice on my shoulder. I look up and see myself reflected in the mirrored surface of his helmet's visor. The blanket falls over my shoulders and head and the stinging of the sand fades. Aeon pulls me to my feet and leads me toward the gangway. The wind pounds our backs, pushing us up toward the open door. I reach out and grasp the pillar. I turn to Aeon. But as I do, he slips. I can't see his face, but I sense his desperation in the way he grips at my arm. But his gloves give him little purchase. His fingers slip, his boots scrape on the gangway and then he is torn away for me.

I watch in horror as he is pulled upward into the sky. Gusts of wind, spinning like a tornado, fling him against the back of the storm like a broken doll.

Then he is gone.

I make it back into the ship. I press the button and the door closes. The forces of nature fade to a distant sound rattling against the hull. I sit with my back against the door and cry.

The ship will never fly again, but the condensers survived the storm. Heart-sore and weary, I pull away the blankets that held the units safe. Aeon's laser cutter, pilfered from his toolbox, fires up at a touch of the button. He always looked after what belonged to him. Guilt washes over me again at the thought.

The cutter sears the condensers free from their cradles. They thump to the ground, moisture leaking out from their collection canisters. I sit the unit up and trickle a handful of sand into the funnel. The turbines grind as they spin, but still water begins to form on the blades. I breathe a sigh of relief. They still work.

I get to my feet and lift the unit to my shoulder. It's heavy, but its value on a world like this is priceless. I look up into the now clear sky. The three suns blaze down on my forehead. I close my eyes then open them again. Time to go. I step away from the ship and head toward the distant horizon. If I am lucky, I will find the aliens we came looking for. Perhaps they might find my gift of water a fair trade for my life. Or perhaps this may be the End of Days for me.

A PITCHER OF WATER AT THE END OF DAYS

As I walk, heading for the far horizon, I am struck by the irony that on this desert planet, I have become what my mother named me for. A woman holding a pitcher of water on her shoulder. I have become Aquarius, the Water Bearer.

About the Author:

Pamela Jeffs is a speculative fiction author living in Queensland, Australia with her husband and two daughters. She is a member of the Queensland Writers' Centre and has had numerous short fiction pieces published in recent national and international anthologies. In 2017 and again in 2018, Pamela was nominated for an Australian Aurealis Award in the category of 'Best Science Fiction Short Story'.

Her debut collection titled Red Hour and Other Strange Tales *was released in March 2018 and her follow up works titled* Saloons and Stardust: A Collection *and* Five Dragons *in 2019. For further information, visit her at* www.pamelajeffs.com

SHE WALKS ON FROSTED FIELDS

Aiki Flinthart

Her bare feet leave no prints in the snow. Her pale body casts no bruised shadow on the field of broken diamonds. She smiles back at me, with teeth white and sharp, and eyes of green ice and darkness. The weak sun turns her white hair into a crown of glittering glass knives.

I must be delirious. There's no other explanation. Altitude sickness. Dehydration.

"You're not real," I mutter, holding on to sanity. "I'm Andrea Chen I live in Sydney. I just have to get off this glacier. Tell people that Michael's dead . . ." I grit my teeth against the lump in my throat. Tears will only steam up my goggles. Guilt is pointless. The best I can do is get to town and find people to retrieve his body.

She gestures with a slender hand and drifts across the glacier like a snowflake. Wafting downhill. Towards the valley, maybe? I've been on the ice so long I can't be sure which way leads to safety. The clouds have turned me in circles. Now they've parted maybe I can find my way out.

She waves again. Urging me on. Such a beautiful figment.

I follow, compelled. She's the first . . . person? . . . I've seen in two days. Light glints off snow. Blue-shadowed, fae light; dimmed by my goggles to bearable levels. Clouds close overhead and dull the anaemic sun.

My chest aches and I press a hand to my side as I hurry to catch up. I shouldn't have come hiking with fractured ribs. But I'd spent months planning this trip. The injury had only made me more determined. I'd missed too much of life, already. No more. I touch my belly. Is the flutter there just my imagination?

My breath mists the air, obscuring the figure gliding away. Panic swells in me. "Wait!" I call. My voice is lost in the vast, broken whiteness; captured and returned distorted by the stony arms imprisoning the glacier.

But she pauses. Gestures. Her long grey skirt sparkles and floats about her ankles like snow. How can she possibly be warm enough? Even in the sun it's barely above freezing.

I squint at the sky and check my watch. Maybe an hour until sundown. The sun abandons the world for longer each night. And half the day it cowers, like a frightened child, behind the black stone ridges that slice the sky on three sides.

I need to pitch my tent soon and get some rest. Eat the last of my rations. I've miscalculated. Michael carried more of the food. His pack is at the bottom of a crevasse.

Clouds thicken and tumble lower in the valley; a tide, surging over the foot of the glacier, swelling up toward me, drowning the world. They smother me and she's gone. I yell a hoarse cooo-eee. Roiling clouds suck the sound from my lips. I'm alone again.

I shove the goggles onto my forehead. Bitter cold stings my eyeballs and tears form. I rub them away and hiss as my clumsy, gloved fingers press against the bruise on my left eye. The week-old cut on my cheek is closed, at least. No stitches needed this time.

I stumble onward, peering at treacherous ground obscured by shifting mists. Ice crunches underfoot with the unsteady rhythm of my steps. In a cocoon of swirling grey, that's the only sound: crunch, crunch, crunch. Steps eating distance, carrying me closer to . . . to where?

I don't know which way to safety. Is there such a thing, anywhere? At any moment I could misstep and plummet to my death. Then the glacier would have two more victims. Three, instead of one. Guilt and despair close my throat and curl around a knot in my stomach.

My thighs burn. My lungs ache in the thin air. My icebound heart drags at heavy feet and a boot catches in a crevasse. I stumble, collapsing into the snows. The backpack lurches forward, pressing my face into the ground. The weight pins me in place. I fist handfuls of snow and crush it into hard lumps. The snow stifles my scream. Cold soaks through my pants, through my jacket, eating into bone and flesh hardened by guilt and grief.

I shatter again. I cannot go on. But I must.

A thousand regrets pin me to the ice. Things I should have said to him. Things I should have done for him. To him. But he's gone.

The glacier speaks in deep groans and creaks. It sang to Michael. He swore he heard voices in the clouds; followed them. Fell. I couldn't stop him. Didn't.

I don't care anymore. The glacier can take me if it wants. Suck me into one of its thousand, groaning mouths—as it did Michael. Chew me up, swallow me into its dark bowels—as it did Michael.

The ice growls at me, echoing my despair, my hope. The fluttering sickness, low in my body, pushes me to rise; to carry on; to start a life after Michael. I roll stiffly and scramble to my knees. Half-healed ribs grind painfully together.

The pale woman . . . creature re-emerges from the swirling cloud, her head cocked to one side, white brows raised. A faint, uncertain smile curls the corners of her pale mouth. She waves me on, urgent, frowning now.

"Who are you?" I call.

She drifts away. I stagger after her. Is this wise? Should I find somewhere sheltered to pitch the tent? But another endless, solitary night huddled around the tiny burner, listening for Michael's voice in the creaking ice holds no appeal. My rations are almost gone. My butane tank almost empty. Without food, I can maybe last another couple of days. Without water, less. My mouth is parched. Surrounded by endless frozen water. Unable to drink. The irony doesn't escape me, but I fail to appreciate it.

On I trudge, tripping over shattered ice, following a broken dream and a fantasy. Is that the faintest sound of laughter? Or true delirium setting in? She glides ahead of me, one with the mist; her outline a blur of wet grey paint on a white canvas.

I follow the snow-sprite. What other choice is there? This is insanity, but so is the entire trip. The madness of the desperate. The desperation of the fearful. The fear of the wounded.

At this point, I have little to lose by following a delusion. But if she saves me, will I be truly saved? Guilt gnaws at my stomach, eating me from the inside out. I miss him. Not what I expected when I started planning this journey three months before. Anticipation, excitement, relief—yes. Not pain and guilt.

The light fades. I stumble on. The air is slightly warmer now. Thicker. With a faint tang of salt. Or that could be my imagination.

Decisions are too hard. They involve thinking, which triggers memories. Walking is easier. No thought required. The adrenalin has long since worn off. The nausea in my stomach after Michael fell is a dull, distant uneasiness. Bearable if I ignore it.

A chasm looms at my feet and I gasp, teetering on the edge, flailing at air not thick enough to grab. Her white head appears from within the gaping crevasse. She points to my right. In the last glimmer of daylight, I make out what seems to be a rough set of stairs, carved in ice. She smiles and nods.

I fumble in my pack and pull out a torch. The stairs are little more than tumbled blocks of ice, arranged and chipped into risers. The brilliant white of my torch illuminates blue walls, smooth and carved into gleaming sculptural curves. The crevasse descends into the body of the glacier. When I look up, the sky is indistinguishable from ice and I'm entombed.

Snowflakes drift down and wind wails an eerie chorus across the opening high above. Too late to go back up. I can't set up the tent in a blizzard. I continue down. The ground levels out and I stamp my crampons so I don't slip on the smooth floor. Chipping away at blue diamond-hardness with teeth of steel.

The walls widen and curve into a hall that appears almost man-made in its perfection. Ice underfoot gives way to grey, tumbled rocks. I unclip the crampons and stuff them into my pack, then tug off my ski-mask. The flutter of a pale skirt ahead draws me on.

A rushing sound overwhelms the glacier's groans and crackles. The roar grows louder. I emerge through an arch, into an enormous cavern of ice. The torchlight plays across a cathedral ceiling carved of glistening concave gouges. Water drips occasionally, but it's lost in the gurgling wash of water tumbling over the stones at my feet. A river, deep under the glacier. Milky blue-green; the colour of blindness.

I fill my water bottle, keeping my gloves out of the icy chill. The water makes my teeth ache, but I gulp it down anyway. And shiver as it hits my stomach.

The tunnel extends beyond my torchlight in both directions. Downriver should lead me out, into the valley and the little town at the foot of the glacier. To questions about Michael's death.

I hesitate and flash the light upstream again. She flinches, raising a hand to shield her eyes from the glare. She seems more substantial down here. Her skin gleaming with moisture. Her dress heavy with damp.

"Sorry," I say, but the word is lost in the waterfall of noise.

She dances lightly from rock to rock, heading upstream. I follow.

Another graceful arch leads to a smaller tunnel that twists into the glacier's belly and emerges into a new cavern. The river is now a muted rumble in the background. The blood of the glacier pumping through its artery. Around me, the ice-bones creak and crackle, complaining of age and unwelcome warmth.

The floor of the cavern is level and reasonably smooth. Warmer and less terrifying than the blizzard raging above. She nods and smiles as I pitch my tent and unroll my sleeping bag. My legs give out and I sit on a rock, head hanging. The relief of being off the glacier after three days sets my body trembling. I hold back a sob with my gloved hand.

I'm dimly aware that I need to eat to help stave off hypothermia. Rummaging in my pack results in two muesli bars and a silverfoil pack of food. I tear open a bar and movement catches my eye. She's still here. Standing just outside the beam of my torch, watching me. I offer her the muesli bar.

She creeps closer and sniffs it. A small nibble and she screws up her nose. Up close her skin is a bluish hue and she has four slits in the skin under her jaw, low behind her ears on each side.

"What's your name?" I ask. I point to myself. "I'm Andrea." I can't believe I'm having a conversation with my hallucination.

Her mouth opens and closes. Squeaks emerge. I shake my head.

"I can't understand." I wave a hand at her, and myself, and at the cavern. "Thank you for this, though. For saving me."

She smiles gently. I hope she understood, but I doubt it. She touches the cut on my cheek. Her fingers are cold and webbed up to the second knuckle. Her green eyes widen. A milky lens, the same colour as the river, sweeps briefly across them. She touches the bruising again. Harder. I pull away with an indrawn hiss.

She cocks her head, frowning.

"Yes," I say wryly, pointing to my yellowing black eye. "Let's just say you have the right idea—living down here alone." I press at my ribs, testing them. The pain isn't any worse than ten days ago when it happened. I'll survive. I lay a hand on my belly and smile for the first time in months.

I open my pack and pull out a small cooking pot. She watches in apparent fascination, following my every movement. I set up the butane stove and empty my last packet of dehydrated unlabelled something into the pot. Stir water in. She screws up her nose again. I sniff the pot. Curry. Again. But I haven't eaten all day and I'll need strength to make it out of here in the morning.

I light the stove. The flame hisses blue-yellow in the arctic darkness. She squeals. So high-pitched it drives through my skull like a hot wire. She vanishes down the hall. I wait but she doesn't come back.

Left alone in the splintering darkness, I eat and try not to think about him. Every time I do, guilt twists at my stomach and I want to beg for his return. But I can't. He's gone. I ache for his guidance. Why wasn't I better? Was it my fault? Did I do the right thing?

I methodically pack away my cooking gear and curl up in my sleeping bag. There, nestled in the womb of the old woman glacier, I rest well. Fear, my bedfellow for over twelve months, has fallen from me.

When I wake my watch says it's six am. Down here the darkness is absolute. I flick the torch on and strike camp. I eat my last muesli bar and drink again. I need to pee, but I don't want to pollute her home. I'll hold it until I reach the river.

I want to say goodbye but she's nowhere to be seen. Not surprising, given she was all in my head. Michael would have known that. He would have set me straight.

I stand at the exit from my shelter and stare into a future with no Michael. A future full of interrogation and tears and endless guilt . . . and hope. A future that cannot be avoided. I need closure and the world will need answers. Demand answers.

Answers to the wrong questions. Questions asked of the wrong person.

Lifting my chin, I shoulder my pack and follow the tunnel back to the river. But I choose the wrong path and step into another chamber. A thin fall of sunlit water cascades through a hole in the ceiling. Diamond drops of light coruscate and dance through the air. A fragile squeal echoes over the noise of water. I swing the torch around and the light bends into a deep, clear pool beneath the waterfall.

Five of my hallucinations float in the water, their white hair swaying like seaweed. They climb from the pool and gather around me. I swallow and hold still as they touch my clothes, my face, my hair. They are smaller than the one who led me to safety. Children of varying heights. Female. Unclothed. All with the same green eyes and webbed fingers.

They don't seem to mean me harm but I back out the door, my heart racing. Not hallucinations. Real. These are real beings. But how?

I can't deal with this. My mind is too full of Michael. He would know what to do. He would tell me what to think about this. I run back down the tunnel. And take another wrong turn. Overhead a narrow crevasse lets watery blue light fall into the tunnel. A huge boulder blocks my path. I swear and turn around.

She's standing silently behind me. I squeak and she flinches, eyes wide.

"Sorry," I say. "I have to go. Can you show me the river?"

She smiles and touches my face, gently. I recoil. I can't help it. She steps past me and leans her shoulder against the stone. Why?

It's too big to move. The rock grinds against the granite underfoot. I edge backward, gaping. The boulder rolls aside, revealing a dark opening. She waves me in.

Hesitant, I flash the torch. Dark piles of what looks like fur lie mounded against the walls. The scent of animal and death wafts out. I'm reluctant to go any further. But she's in there, waving me on. I step in, half-expecting the door to rumble closed. It stays open.

I pan the torch around. The light wavers in my hand. Curled against a rock, a man lifts his head and blinks. Hopeful fear lights his face and he holds up a hand, squinting.

"Who's there?" His voice is thin and quavery, made old-mannish in his fear. His blond hair lank and oily. Blue eyes shadowed with sleeplessness and pain.

She urges me in. I resist, trembling. The torch falls from my hand, tumbling and dancing over the rocky floor. It's unbreakable, unlike me. It comes to rest with the light shining in my face.

"Andrea! Thank God! Get me out of here." Michael's voice takes on the command tones I'm used to, and my feet move of their own accord. Two steps towards him.

I stop, torn. Ripped asunder. I want him. But he's gone. I was almost used to the idea.

"Andrea." He sounds confident. Certain of me.

I collect the torch and shine it on him again. She stands before him, one hand pressed against his chest. She's looking at me. There's an unmistakable question in those green eyes.

"Andy? C'mon, sweetheart." That wheedling tone gets under my defences. "You have no idea how glad I am to see you! I told you this trip was a bad idea. Dunno why you were so dead set on it. But I came, right? Now let's go home. I promise I won't be mad at you."

He loves me. I know he does. I take another step towards him. He nods, eager.

"When I fell into that crevasse, I thought this . . . this . . ."

"Woman," I say.

"Whatever." He dismisses her with a flick of a hand. "I thought it was rescuing me. But it dragged me down here. I thought I was a goner."

She cocks her head and utters a sharp, lilting creel. She's still looking at me, still pinning Michael to the wall. Michael shoves at the arm holding him in place.

She doesn't move. Isn't affected. He's taller and broader in the shoulder but she holds him like he's half her size. His brow clouds and I cringe back.

"Let me go, you bitch!" He swings at her, fist balled, aiming for the cheek.

She blocks his arm with casual ease. Slaps him so hard his knees sag and he half-slips down the boulder face. His eyes roll back and he groans. She straightens and dusts her hands.

Looking in my direction, she points at Michael. Then at herself. Her hands outline a lump over her belly. Then she mimes rocking a baby in her arms and smiles, crooning.

Michael groans. His hands flex and curl into fists again.

"Andy." My name emerges thick from his bloodied mouth. He scowls. "Don't piss me off. No more games. Just call it off and get me out of here."

My ribs twinge. The cut under my eye throbs. I stay where I am.

He regains some of his power and straightens. Wiping at his mouth, he sees the blood and grimaces. "See what it did to me?" He touches a fingertip to the cut on his cheek again, anger gathering in his eyes. And just a hint of fear.

I shiver. I recognise that look.

Her lips draw back in a knowing smile and she leans closer to him. Michael recoils. She casts a knowing, glittering grin over her shoulder at me. She touches the cut on his face, then the same spot on her own cheek, leaving a dab of scarlet on her pale skin. Then she points at me, and at the door.

"Andrea!" Disbelief tinges his cry.

I hesitate. All the early days of our time together flood into me, filling me with the memory of warmth and laughter. Then the torchlight catches the crimson spot on her face, and on his. My fractured cheekbone aches. The child in me is a little storm; a sickness in my stomach at the promise in Michael's eyes.

I swing the torch around the chamber. Michael's not the only inhabitant; just the only living one. The piles of fur are eight mummified bodies. They lie against the walls, curled into foetal positions. I light up Michael again. His eyes are wide, stark.

"Michael," I say, rolling his name on my tongue, tasting it again. "Did you know that eight men have gone missing on this glacier in the last twenty years?"

"What the hell are you talking about? Get her off me, damn you." He shoves at her arm again.

I back away. The chamber opening is right behind me. The river's breeze tosses hair into my eyes. Cool, fresh, clean. Water rushing towards the ocean.

"Do you know what the locals call this glacier, Michael?" I ask.

"What the hell? Stop blathering. Get back here! Andy!"

I'm outside the chamber, standing free of darkness, bathed in light.

"The Widowmaker," I say. "They call this glacier the Widowmaker."

About the Author:

Aiki Flinthart has 13 published novels and one non-fiction book, along with numerous short stories published in various anthologies and e-magazines. Her stories have been shortlisted in the Australian Aurealis Awards and she has been twice a top-8 finalist in the USA Writers of the Future competition.

When not writing, Aiki likes to practice fantasy-approved hobbies such as martial arts, archery, knife-throwing, lute-playing, and belly-dancing. You can find her on Facebook, Twitter, and Instagram—she's the only Aiki Flinthart—and here: www.aikiflinthart.com

TRIDENT'S SONG

Nikky Lee

The Muses say a voice is the song of the soul. If that's true, then my soul is rotten.

I dart across the rocks, dodging swirling water as it rushes in from the sea. Kelp pops underfoot, like Aunt Ligea's cackle when she saw the ship round the headland of our island in the midday sun.

"Go see to it," she'd instructed, stabbing a gnarled finger in the direction of the cliffs, before hobbling off to join her sister in the kitchen. "Get the hearth going!" she called to Menesmy.

Down on the sand, the chiming of pots and cutlery still rings in my ears. I reach the end of the beach and clamber up over the limestone headland. Pebbles and spiky grass stab at my feet, and I hop, curse, and press on, ignoring the drop of the cliff and the crash of the sea below.

Ahead, the mast of my quarry rounds the peninsula. I scurry after it, chasing it like a fox after a rabbit, wind pushing at my back, urging me on. A few more steps and they'll be in my reach. My voice is not that of my aunties', but with the wind to carry it, it will be enough.

I come over the rise and the cliffs give way to Mercies Bay, all tumbled rock and white sand. The ship is dropping anchor. Doubled over, I take two full breaths, let my heart slow, lungs ease. Then I straighten, throw my head back, and sing.

My screech echoes down the clifftops. On the ship's deck, men jump, like mice startling at the kee of a hawk. Someone shouts, a few try to cover their ears, but already the crew are laxing still, eyes glazing as they listen. Their faces turn up to my cliff.

Come. I silently entreat. *A feast awaits.*

Slowly, one by one, they move. A shuffle, bumping shamble, like a herd of sleepwalkers. Their hands find the pulleys and ropes that drop their skiffs into the water and then the oars to row them ashore.

I meet them on the beach, still humming under my breath—if you could call my rasping notes a hum. *"If a snake could sing, it'd sound like you,"* Aunt Ligea had once said.

No matter, it does the job. I march our fare off the beach, humming them down the goat tracks to our cave and into the pens. Only when Aunt Menesmy swings the bars shut and I let my song die, do they blink, owl-like in the dim, and take stock of the damp rock walls and the cell door.

All too late.

Like the others before them, they fling themselves at the bars, cries erupting off the stone, ringing in my ears.

"Hush," Menesmy sings, her voice rising above them, sharp and honed as a knife. "Hush my lovelies." The barbs of power in her notes silence them, and they sway, like chickens settling into their coop, oblivious to the fate awaiting them on the other side of the door.

I scuttle into the kitchen before the power of her song dies and they start clucking again. Aunt Ligea looks up from the stone slab that serves as her carving stable, iron blade in her hand.

"Get the pit started, Fídi," she snaps, thrusting her knife at the flint box by the hearth. When I hesitate, her eyes sharpen on me, as if wondering whether to carve out my innards along with our catch.

The hunger is in her. Best not to argue while she's like this. I swallow my question, scoop up the flint box and climb the stairs. Up and out onto the headland, to the fire pit among the limestone and salt-blasted olive trees. Two twisted trees, old as my aunts, hunch over the coals, the log of a spit slung between them. Story goes, according to Menesmy, that she and Ligea each sang one up from a seed.

I've only seen them work power over men. Sometimes, when they're hungry and not seen sight of a ship in months, they try to work their magic on me; a faint vibrato that curls off their words, and every now and then a sentence that slides into near melody. A test, checking yet again if their tone-deaf niece might not have enough human in her worth eating.

Yet I remain impervious as ever. My mother's blood, what little I have, runs in me: too weak to wield the same power as they, but strong enough to resist it. So I stay. A snake, Fídi, who sulks at the edge of their cave, song like a serpent's hiss.

The flames are hot and high when a squeal ricochets up from the cave below. My hairs prickle, they do every time. The sound is quickly silenced; a flash of Ligea's knives probably. I hurry, throwing more logs onto the pit, and fan the flames, sending them skyward so that when they calm, my aunts will have hot coals to work with.

Menesmy and Ligea come to the fire, hunched over like their two olive trees. The sailor's body weighs them down; hollowed and naked, and marinated in salt and sage. My aunts are not the young sirens they once were. Once, Ligea tells, they were as hawks—strong and straight-backed, chests proud. A force of nature.

Now they are vultures. Picking the bones of their island dry.

They would escape if they could, but our bloodline is bound to this earth by a witch. Cursed never to leave until we know love. That was how my mother escaped. And also how she died, so my aunts tell me.

"Love is death," Menesmy said years ago, eyes hungry on the horizon as if waiting for something more than men to come to our shores; Charon's wooden boat, perhaps, come to whisk her heart away to the underworld. "You must never love, Fídi." This advice was as close to kindness as my aunts ever came. I'd nodded, thinking of the years she'd been trapped here. The years more that lay here for me. Because who would ever love a snake?

Aunt Ligea turns the spit; the meat bubbles and hisses, dropping fat into the coals. Menesmy hovers at her shoulder, flecks of red in the hem of her apron. Smoke hazes the air, thick and musky, and Ligea and Menesmy stare into the fire and grin at one another. The scent descends the stair and the voices of the soon-to-be-dead rise from the cave:

"Monsters." "Release us." The wind tosses their words to the waves beating the cliffs below.

Ligea huffs and jabs a finger at me, nail long as an eagle's talon. "Go feed them."

It's no accident my aunts have forgotten to throw them their scraps. This is how it goes. Every time they find some excuse to send me away before I can share in the spoils. But this time, I hesitate. This time I had been the one who met our fare on the shore and sang them into their pens. Had I not earned my place with them? Ligea jabs the air again, glaring. "Go on. Get!"

Apparently not. Snakes, it seems, do not dine with hawks.

With one last look at the spit and the twisted trees, I leave.

The oars are heavy as I pull them through the water, an uncomfortable burn simmering between my shoulder blades and along my arms. The little rowboat lurches forward in the chop again. Ahead, the sailors' empty ship looms, creaking and swaying with the sea.

"Fetch their stores, before it all goes to seed," Aunt Ligea had snapped by way of a morning greeting when I'd entered the kitchen for breakfast. Again, I'd hesitated, eyes landing on her bloated belly, round as a nesting hen's, and felt the empty pinch of my own stomach.

"What are you waiting for? Go on," Ligea had shooed a hand at me. "And be quick about it." But my attention lingered on the dried fruits Menesmy was preparing beside her sister, desperately hoping for eye contact, a bone, some measure of affection. Idiot that I was. Ligea's fingers had curled around my shoulder, biting deep. "Don't make me raise my voice," she'd cooed in my ear.

I'd nodded and made a quick retreat.

"Lazy snake," Ligea had muttered as I rounded the stair, before reciting her favourite barb, the one she uses when she knows I'm still in earshot. "Tell me again, why can't we eat her?"

"Hush, Ligea," this from Mesnemy. "We do not eat our own."

I pull the oars again, anger lending me strength. One day, I'd find a way off this cursed land. It's an old oath, a mantra I repeat under my breath when Ligea's taunting or Menesmy's disinterest gets the better of my temper. Like today. One day, I swear, I'll leave.

My rowboat comes to a rest against the ship with a gentle thud. She's low in the water, her hold full. No wonder Ligea lusts after it. I stow the oars and rise from the seat, but too fast and set the rowboat pitching. My heart pounces into my ribs, and I grapple for a hold, knuckles white on the boat's rim.

Never go in the water. Menesmy's warning rings in my head. *We are of the air. Poseidon and his ilk don't take kindly to trespassers. Enter the sea and they will snare you, pull you into the deep where you will rot. Trapped forever, never to see the sky again.* My aunt's face looms out of my memory, black eyes boring into mine. *Do you want that, Fidi?*

No, I'd squeaked.

The rocking eases. I release my breath and curse my carelessness. When I stand again, it's more of a crouch, stance wide, knees bent as I fetch my rope and grapple. After a few attempts, it catches on the rail and I clamber up. The deck is quiet, nothing but the faint hum of the wind in the rigging.

I throw open the hold and examine the cargo. Rows of amphorae pots are stacked inside, lashed together with rope and with straw stuffed between them to stop them breaking. Painted figurines on their sides shift in the light, in time with the buck and sway of the ship. I grab the first, sniff the seal once. Grain. The same for the next. The third sloshes when I haul it frec—a bitter, sweet scent. Wine. I put it to one side. My aunts will never come out here to check the hold themselves. They dare not cross the water. And a single crock of wine won't be missed.

Deeper in the hold, something clunks; one full pot falling onto another. I start, head snapping up, and I squint into the dim. Nothing moves. My eyes narrow. Someone is here. I know it in my gut. The same way I know when my song snares a human. I dig my nails into the seal of the first amphora, pull the lid and spill the contents out. Then I grab the handles and raise the empty crock above my head, ready to strike.

"Come out," I say, then curse myself for a fool. "Show yourself." I push my will into the words. They wheeze out in a rasp.

No movement. No sense of a mind ensnaring.

I frown, shuffle forward, empty crock raised.

A shadow flits to my right. I round on it, catch a glimpse of eyes and a mouth open in a silent scream. It trips, gangly limbs sprawling into a row of pots, sending them tumbling. I yelp and swing my crock down, cracking it over its head with a tinkle of breaking terracotta. The limbs flop, eyes roll back into its head.

Silence fills the hold.

Swallowing my thumping heart, I lower the shattered crock and peer at my prey. Human. Out cold. I mutter a word of thanks to the Anemoi—gods of the winds—and move closer, then cock my head, suddenly unsure of my initial assessment. Where the men I snared from this ship were broad and thick-necked from working the oars, this one is smaller, knees knobbled as a newborn goat's, and thin. Bare skin stretches tight over ribs like hide over a drum. So thin not even aunt Ligea would eat him.

But you could. The thought freezes me on the spot. Could I? My aunts assumed I'd rounded up all the sailors, they didn't know I'd missed one. And what they didn't know . . .

My hollow stomach emits a growl. *Do it,* my hunger wills. Fill the emptiness. Feast. Taste a man's flesh, just once. Ligea and Menesmy will never know.

I fumble for a shard of broken amphora. The piece my fingers wrap around is long and jagged and digs into my skin. I nudge the human with a toe. A groan. Not deep like the voices in our pen, but high and scratchy. Like mine. My gut clenches. I teeter, makeshift knife raised above my head. *Do it.*

But then his eyes open, deep brown and dazed, and suddenly I'm the one sprawled on the ground as a memory of Ligea towers over me, her fists bunched.

"Idiot snake," she'd barked. *"Give it here."*

In my hands, I cupped a songbird, feathers still downy from the nest. One of its wings was bent. I'd found it like that under the olive trees, beak slightly ajar and eyes glazed from the fall.

"Give it," Ligea had spat. Reluctantly, I had. And in less than a heartbeat, her talons curled around the bird's neck and snapped it dead. She handed the body back to me. *"We have enough vermin in our den. Get rid of it."*

In the ship's hold, my resolve wavers. My stomach gurgles, but my arms won't move.

And the boy stares at me, hair crusted into salty whorls, cheeks as pinched as my stomach. Hungry, just like me. Something flashes behind his eyes. Fear. *Just like mine.*

It's like watching a reflection.

My resolution breaks. I can't. I put the shard-knife down, arms trembling as if I'd hefted an axe twice my size. "Can you stand?" I ask.

He stares at me, blank-faced. For a moment, I wonder if he doesn't speak Mycenaean. I scrounge together my limited Doric and ask again. Same response. Could be he's from further east, Anatolia perhaps, though that doesn't help me. My aunts have never seen, let alone wooed, an Anatolian ship—not in my lifetime at least. I revert back to Mycenaean, turning my words slow, pushing power into them again, transcending language.

"Tell me your name."

But the words run off him like water. He blinks at me. I purse my lips. I might be a candle to my aunts' bonfire, but I have power enough to know when it's working. Or should be working. And yet it doesn't. Nothing is going to plan today.

"Caleus." The word comes too loud for the quiet hold. "I am Caleus."

So, he does speak Mycenaean. But it's nasally, accented in a way I can't place. He pushes himself onto his elbows and taps a hand to his bare chest. "Caleus."

I scowl. "I heard you the first time." I pick up an unbroken amphora from its row. It's heavy, full of more wine, and I lug it over to the stepladder. "Make yourself useful and help me carry these."

He doesn't move. Just peers at me, a furrow working across his dark brow. "Caleus," I say, slowly, looking him dead in the eye. He straightens, nods, almost enthusiastic.

I point to the rows of amphorae. "Carry . . . the . . . pots." I wince as the words leave me. It's the same tone Ligea uses when I don't do a chore quick enough or to her liking. Ridiculing. Stripping all sense of worth away as she might the skin off a goat.

But Caleus brightens, face lighting up, understanding. Is he simple? I'd seen men like that before in my aunt's caves. They'd not lasted long. Their crewmates had pushed them to the front of the pen, offering them up first. For some reason, the sight of it had always set my blood boiling.

For his part, Caleus nods to himself again and scoops up a pot. He carries it up the ladder, crosses the deck in long confident strides, holding the pot with ease, as if he'd been doing it all his life. Perhaps he has. Though, if he is one of the crew, he is a far cry from the men penned up in my aunt's cave. Feet and chest bare, and nothing but a wrapped linen skirt around his waist. And thin as a sapling. Though how he'd come to be so, with all that food and grain around him in the hold, was beyond me. Perhaps he hadn't dared eat it, even with the crew gone. The same way I didn't dare to steal a sliver of meat from my aunt's fire pit. I'd always sensed that somehow they'd know, find out, and then I'd be in for a reckoning that would make Hades shudder.

Caleus thumps the pot down beside the ship rail and peers over the side at the rowboat, head tilting as he considers the best way down. He moves along the rail, finds a loose rope and gathers it, weighing it in rough hands before tying it around the neck of the amphorae. With a clatter of terracotta on wood, he lowers the pot over the side of the ship.

I blink. Not a simpleton then. So, how did he escape my song?

Caleus steps one foot onto the railing, as if about to leap off into the sea. Panic seizes my chest. Is he trying to kill himself? Menesmy's warning fills my ears. *Poseidon will pull you into the deep where you will rot.* Cold rushes up my arms, twists in my belly. I wouldn't wish that fate on anyone.

"Wait!" I fling the word at him, my power turning my voice hoarse. But my song slides off him. He doesn't pause. Doesn't so much as twitch at my rasp. And with a flash of sun-tanned skin and linen skirt, he's over. Jumped. And water droplets splash over the deck from below.

Gods be.

I run to the side, heart in my mouth, and there he is, unharmed and streaking through the water like a porpoise.

In two strokes, he's at my boat, water splattering the planks as he pulls himself in. Horror seizes me. He's going to steal my skiff; leave me trapped on this dead ship. Power swells in my throat, and I grip the rail, nails digging into the wood. "Don't you dare."

He doesn't listen. Doesn't even deem to hear. *How? Why* doesn't it work?

"Caelus," I say, panic rising as he shifts around in the boat below. No response. "Caelus!"

He reaches for his amphora, twists the knot free about its neck, and releases the rope. He flings it loose, looking to me once more with a grin, motioning me to haul the rope back up.

Then it hits me. "You're deaf."

Caelus frowns, cups a hand over his eyes and squints at me. When I make no sound, no movement, he flicks the rope and motions again, miming me pulling it up hand over hand and wind it around the pot I'm carrying. Something in the jerk and sway of the gestures suggests impatience, as if he's saying, *hurry up, can't you see I'm waiting?*

Deaf. My power won't work on him. I swallow. Nothing to stop him doing what the men in the cave often threaten, once they realise begging doesn't work. And now it was too late, I'd let him live. I glance down. But not all humans in the pen had been violent. Some had been kind, an intuition in them had sensed that while not in the cage with them, I was as trapped as they.

My hands find the rope, winds it around the pot, and lowers it over the side. Below, Caleus unties it and stashes it next to the first. I run and fetch another pot, then another, and another, lowing each in turn. After the tenth, Caelus throws up a palm. *Stop.* Then he waves at me: a beckoning to come down.

I hesitate, the thought of crossing over the sea with a virtual stranger twisting in my stomach. One push and I'd be dead. Caught in Poseidon's grip. The hairs rise on my arms . . .

Where you will rot . . . I swallow.

Caleus raises an eyebrow, folds his arms and makes a show of tapping his foot. *Well?*

My eyes rove over him. Skin and bones and human. But different.

Like me.

Gods curse it, if this decision gets me killed . . . I clamber down, chafing my palms as I go. Caleus moves over on the skiff's wooden bench and takes up an oar. Squashing my misgivings, I do the same on the other side.

The row to shore is uneventful, though Caleus tires quickly. It's not long before he's wheezing beside me, but he refuses to let me take his oar, as if determined to earn his passage. A scrape of wood on sand and pebble and we hit the beach, I crouch on the bench preparing to leap over the water to the safety of the shore and pull the boat in by its rope. But before I can motion at Caleus to stay put, he's in the water again, up to his knees, hauling the nose of the boat higher up the beach.

Then the prow wedges, unable to go further, and he staggers away, sprawling onto the dry sand above the tideline, chest rising and falling. I open my mouth, words already forming in my head to call him back, only to stop, remembering he won't hear. Not that he's looking my way at all. His eyes are shut; fingers curled into the sand as if in some strange prayer. Perhaps he thought he'd die on that ship. While he might have had food a plenty in those amphorae, I hadn't found any that contained fresh water.

I dig my grappling rope into the sand and go over to him. And stare.

He's fast asleep.

I hide him in one of the sea caves at the furthest end of the bay. My aunts rarely venture far from our cave, not unless there's a quarry to catch. And with the sailors in the pens, eight at my last count, Ligea and Menesmy would not leave. My aunts like their comforts; Menesmy her woven chair beside the hearth and Ligea her long couch draped in animal furs.

At first, I tried to bring Caleus food from my aunts' table. But when Ligea caught me saving my scraps, she fed the bowl to the sailors below.

"If you don't want them, they will," she said. "Zeus knows they need a bit of fattening before the pit."

Menesmy had watched it all without comment, as always, her gnarled fingers working her loom with a mind of their own.

So I returned to the ship, taking Caleus with me, and each day we shuttle two boatloads of amphorae onto the beach. One goes onto the little hand-drawn cart that I pull back over the cliffs to my aunts. The other I leave in Caleus' cave.

"Don't worry," I tell Caleus when we unload the last of it a week after our first meeting. He frowns at the stacks of amphorae pushed up against the cave's limestone wall. "They're not coming back. You can eat from them."

I make sure to look at him when I speak. I'd discovered that so long as I face him, he can see the words on my lips. His frown deepens, hands laxing to his sides. His gaze lingers on my face, eyes catching mine before they dart, once, back to the ship anchored in the bay, expressive in a way I've never seen. I understand his meaning at once.

How can you be sure?

I shrug, keen to avoid the topic. "Trust me, they won't."

He scowls. Eyebrows flattening to a line. *Liar.*

I sigh. "Just eat."

Those dark eyes stay on me a heartbeat longer, until he huffs and moves off to rekindle his fire of driftwood and bracken. He cooks a portion of the grain, turning it into a burnt slop that sticks to the pot he'd taken from the ship on our last trip over. When it's done, he scoops it into two bowls, also from the ship, and offers me one.

I shake my head, eyeing his knobbly limbs. "I've already eaten." I had. Back at my aunts'. "You need it more than me."

I stand to leave. Stay too long and my aunts will grow suspicious. Well, Ligea will. I doubt Menesmy would care. Caleus starts up from the fire, rising with me. He taps his chest. "Caleus," he says, the only thing I've ever heard him say, then mimes two people walking with his fingers. I shake my head.

"No, you stay here."

His eyebrows flicker. *But–*

"It's not safe."

One eyebrow arches, disbelieving.

"It's not." Gods, if he follows me back, Ligea would snap his neck. And mine. Cold prickles in my gut. Somehow, the idea feels wrong. I swallow, clench my fists. "Stay here." As always, my voice rebounds off him. He blinks, but something must sink in. His ridiculing eyebrow settles, and he looks earnest into my face. *You're serious?*

"Yes. I'm serious." *By the gods I wish I weren't.* "There are . . ." I hesitate, "others here."

He pinches the end of a lock of my hair and holds it up between us, questioning. It's curled, like a snake, and mottled green; so unlike the fine threads my aunts flaunt. Where their heads are white and grey like feathered down, mine is the colour of kelp. I pull my hair free. "Not like me. Bad people. They'll hurt you if they see you."

Caleus' eyes study me a long moment, weighing my words. At last he nods.

When I leave, the knot in my belly doesn't fade.

Three months later, Ligea leans across the table and sniffs. "You smell like human," she says, and my heart thuds into my throat. "Human and—" her thin nose twitches, as if she has an itch, and it's all I can do not to flinch, *"salt."*

I force my voice steady, hoping she can't hear the strain of my guts knotting like a sailor's rope. "I just took the scraps down." True. I always make an excuse to go to the pens after visiting

Caleus' cave. There's only three of them left now. Soon, I'll have to come up with another excuse.

Ligea prowls around the table, nails scratching on stone. "You've been sneaking off a lot lately." Her head snaps close, breath tickling down my neck and she sniffs again. "Back to that ship is it?" Her hand unfurls, palm up. "Give it here."

I hang my head and dig one hand into a pocket, pulling out the driftwood charm Caleus had pushed into my hands a few days earlier. He'd not let me leave without it, eyes earnest when I tried to hand it back. His lips had worked, shaping two words several times until he put his voice behind them:

"Keep safe."

Like a bit of driftwood could protect me from my aunt's wrath. I should have thrown it away. But its weight in my pocket had been comforting as I climbed back up the cliffs to face another day with my aunts. A pebble of hope made just for me.

Ligea snatches the charm up. Turns it over. The symbol of Poseidon flashes into view, the triple trident scored into the wood in careful cuts from Caleus' knife. (I'd swiped the blade from my aunts' table weeks ago after watching him try to whittle a carving with a piece of limestone. Luckily for me, Menesmy assumed she'd misplaced it and made another.)

Ligea shrieks and drops the charm. It bounces across the table. Strange. Menesmy, in an unusual fit of responsiveness, shoots up from her loom spitting curses, saliva frothing on her lips as if she'd just sipped poison. With a flick of her loom needle, she swats the charm into the fire and rounds on me.

"You dare to bring the sea into our home?" Her voice is low, melodious, power pulsing through every syllable. I blink, bewildered. I've grown used to Ligea's scolding, but this is something new. This is a Menesmy I've not seen before. Why so much fuss over a silly trinket? Poseidon can't reach us here. *Or can he?* Gooseflesh shivers up my arms. Menesmy hums another note and her song pushes against my skin, into my ears. For the first time since I can remember, my muscles twitch at its sound. I fight for composure and force the panic down. *Lie, Fidi, lie like your life depends on it.*

Perhaps it does.

"I found it on the ship, I thought it harmless . . ." I stop, hearing the tremolo in my words, some unconscious power working to preserve itself. I swallow, waiting for my aunties to notice.

Only they don't. My power slides off them like it does with Caleus. Weak. Wheezy. *Useless.* I might as well not have a voice at all. A new thought occurs to me, one that turns my bowels to water. Is my power fading? My mother's influence slowly wearing off? Is that what they smell? Am I becoming more human?

Ligea pushes in front of her sister and shoves a honed nail into my face.

"You'll send that ship away," she says. "Sink it, set it a-sail. Get rid of it. Tomorrow."

My heart sinks. I'd had plans for that ship. I had a Caelus hidden on the beach, and he knew how to sail. All I needed was a few months to stockpile enough food away from my aunt's notice. Then we'd take that ship and travel it far away from this wretched island. And if Goddess Tyche and her luck were with us, I'd do it all without ever touching the water.

Ligea leans in, so close her crooked nose almost touches my cheek. "Do it, or . . ."

She leaves the threat unsaid. But there's no missing her hunger. And with a lurch, I recall it's been a month since their last feast. I swallow. Human and salt. *At last, their snake is seasoned and ready.* The thought turns my blood cold. Was that what they'd been waiting for all along? My flesh to turn human? The sweetest meat of all. I try to calm my racing thoughts. They can't, won't. Not yet. There are still three sailors below. Easy pickings.

As if reading my thought, Ligea's finger swings away, pointing to the stairs. "Go prepare the pit."

I go, and it feels like I'm building my own pyre.

We watch the ship round the peninsula, bobbing in the waves. The wind catches its half-strung sail and it rolls and pitches. I've half a mind it will sail past the horizon, but Caleus is convinced it will smash itself to pieces on the cliffs.

Turns out, he's right. A gust of wind whips the ship's prow towards the sheer limestone and the current does the rest.

Splintering groans echo up the beach as the waves break its body on the rocks.

"You're not as bothered about it as I thought you'd be," I tell Caleus when we're back in his cave, warming up a pot of gruel at his fire. "That was your way home." He studies my face as I talk, slowing his stirring of the grain until he wipes his hands, picks up a cold piece of charcoal from the edge of fire and moves to the wall.

Too big to sail alone. He scrawls in a large, untidy hand; a fresh line on our wall of conversations. *Changes nothing.*

"Oh." The thought had never occurred to me. And suddenly I feel stupid for not realising it sooner. Why else would a ship that size have so many crew? I stare up at the dozens upon dozens of sentences, each one dancing in the fire light. I'd taught him the letters to give him something to pass the time, but I'd never expected him to take to them so well.

Caleus taps the wall, pointing to a fresh line squeezed in between a conversation we'd had about where he'd come from (Knossos it turns out) and how he'd come to be on the ship in the first place (not knowing what to do with him, his parents had sold him to the captain as a deckhand when he was seven).

We need something smaller.

"But where would we find something like that?"

He flashes me one of his grins, picks up a flaming stick from the fire, and motions for me to follow. He leads me deeper into the cave and I can't help but glance at it the dwindling store of amphorae as we pass. Two pots remain. And I'm sure one of them is wine. If he rations that last amphora, he has about a week of food left. Then what? If he starts hunting on the island, he risks running into my aunts. One fresh track left behind is all it would take for them to find him.

At the thought of preparing the pit for a spit carrying Caleus, my chest turns suddenly tight. So tight it's hard to breathe. I pull my thoughts away, put a hand to the wall to steady myself. *Breathe.* They won't find him. So long as he stays on the beach. Close to the sea where my aunts fear to tread.

A cough from Caleus snaps my head up. He sweeps out his torch, shining light over the back of the cave. Gods be.

Somehow, when I wasn't looking, he'd gone and built himself a raft.

Driftwood and the remains of two skiffs are lashed together with the ropes from the ship and amphorae. Caleus points out a swathe of ship's sail he's used to create his own smaller version using an oar lashed near the raft's centre as a mast. He steps onto the deck and jumps. The raft bounces, but no ropes snap and the wood doesn't bow under his weight—not that he has much. Hands on hips, he puffs out his chest. *See, it's sturdy.*

I stare. "You can't be serious."

Caleus folds his arms, juts his chin.

He is.

I run my gaze over it again, shake my head. "It'll never work." If the wind and current could smash a ship twenty times the size of this to splinters, it'd have no trouble with Caleus' creation, sturdy or not.

He stamps his foot, grabbing my attention again. *It will!*

I sigh and turn back to the fire.

Caleus follows and as soon as we're back within the halo of the flames, he's writing on the wall. *It's not finished yet.*

"Clearly, there are still holes in the bottom."

He rolls his eyes at me, spins on the wall again. *It's supposed to have holes. The water needs to drain.* His stick of charcoal pauses, and then, slower, he scratches. *Don't you want to leave?*

I sit up, I had never said anything about leaving the island to Caleus. But, somehow, he knew. When had that happened? I cast my thoughts back. Had he always known? Picked up the cues I'd never said aloud?

My gaze drifts to the back of the cave. He was better at reading me than I'd given him credit for. "I can't."

A tightening of the jaw. Angry tapping on the wall. *Why not?*

I flounder, trying to find a way to explain. "I can't . . . swim."

I will teach you.

"No, you don't understand. I *can't.* For me the sea is . . ." I search for the right words, mouth dry at the thought of setting sail on that death trap. "Dangerous." I fix my eyes on his, then enunciate the next two syllables. "Lethal."

Caleus' fist tightens around the charcoal. With a 'plick', it snaps. Then, without warning, he spins and stomps out of the cave.

"Caleus," I call after his retreating back, curse when he doesn't hear, and run after him.

I catch him on the beach. He's ankle deep in the water and stoops to the waves, bowl in hand. When had he grabbed that? He scoops the bowl through the water, then paces up to me at the tideline.

"Caleus," I begin, hoping to explain. Curse it, he's not looking at my face. I grab his shoulder, try to get him to meet my eyes.

He pours the bowl over my head, dousing my hair and face in seawater.

I shriek. So loud, I see the gooseflesh ripple up his arms. He stumbles back, wide eyed, mouth open in that silent scream again. I claw at my hair, expecting pain to bloom across my scalp and run fire down the path the salt has taken. I blink. There's no pain. No fire.

I check myself. I'm fine. Everything is fine. But how can that be? The sea is our enemy. It killed my mother; it should harm me too.

But it hasn't.

I shake my head. I'm mistaken. Must be. I haven't been exposed enough. As soon as I think it, I have to test it. I stagger to the water's edge, hesitate a heartbeat, then step in.

It . . . tingles? I stare at my toes through the white foam. I'd always imagined the sea to be deathly cold, cold like the Stix. But here, it's warm. I push in deeper, up to my knees. The water swirls around my calves, a gentle push-pull against my skirts.

Somewhere inside me, that pinched emptiness I'd always thought was hunger, eases. It feels right.

But how could that be? The sea is dangerous. *It will pull you into the deep.* That's what my aunts always said. Over and over. All my life I'd felt their fear when they'd spoken of the ocean, how they've avoided going near it if they could help it. I'd never thought to question.

A choke from the beach snaps me back to myself. Caleus sits, hunched over and rocking at the tideline. Oh no. I splash out of the water and go to him.

"I'm sorry," I say, but he waves me off, shoulders shaking.

He presses a finger to the sand. It's trembling. *I heard you,* he writes, pauses, digs his index in again. *I <u>felt</u> it.*

And without warning, his arms are around me, hugging me close.

Not sobbing, I realise.

Laughing.

That night, I dream of the sea. Wild visions of waves crashing against the cliffs, gurgling in rockpools, and the strange silence of an ocean floor. I hang below the waterline, weightless, sand eddying in circles below my toes. It's quiet, the wind and rage of the world above muted.

Is this how Caleus experiences the world? The thought drifts through my dreamscape. My mind latches onto it, imagining a waking world underwater. Envying its silence, the freedom of not hearing my aunts send men down to Hades; the comfort of knowing that nothing they sing will ever steal my mind. The thoughts pull me from the dream, and I rise, buoyant, as my mind starts its turning again.

Last night, Caleus shook my arms, half-crying, half laughing. For the first time in his life, he'd experienced sound. To him, my hoarse, wretched shriek had been beautiful. Snatched his breath away, he'd described in shaking letters. I'd wanted to correct him, tell him that what I have is a curse. A voice too weak for siren-kind and too powerful for human. A voice that doesn't belong.

A pot bangs above my head, and Ligea's words dig into me like splinters. "Get up, lazy Fídi. The hearth needs starting."

I open my eyes to the rough walls of my aunt's cave and the cold coals of the hearth. When I don't move quick enough, Ligea cracks her spoon against the pot again. I wince, shielding my ears. Funny, here I am, lying here desperate not to hear, while down on the beach in another cave lies a boy who's desperate to hear more.

"Serves you right for running off so late," Ligea sneers, then stops, spying my skirts drying over the hearth grate. Her eyes narrow. "Why are your skirts wet?"

I scramble up, snatching my clothes. The hems are still damp, but I pull them on. "I went to the spring," I lie. "It was dark, I slipped. Put a foot in."

Would you sing for me tomorrow? Caleus had asked on the beach. *Sing with all your strength so I can hear?* A bad idea, I knew. If my aunts heard, they might get curious. Yet, I'd nodded.

Ligea's leans in. Sniffs, and wrinkles her nose. "Furies should have pushed you all the way. You reek," her index jabs at the stairs. "Go bathe. At once. I'll not have my kitchen smelling like the pens."

My legs stiffen and I fight not to suck in a breath. I'd not visited the pens last night. I'd wandered back in a daze, mind churning, legs still tingling from the push-pull of the surf. I'd forgotten to take the scraps to the two sailors still down there.

I recall the press of Caleus' hug, how his warmth had spread from him to me and the tears of joy soaking into my shoulder. No one had ever held me like that. Ice crawls across my skin. Ligea could smell him. *Idiot, Fídi.* If Ligea went down the pens, saw their scrap bucket still there, she'd catch me in my lie.

"I'll go at once," I croak, and scurry away, heading for the stair.

"Fídi, where are you going?" Menesmy asks from her loom.

I teeter on the step. "To feed them," I say. "Before I bathe."

A long silence, and my gut twists tighter and tighter, until at last, Menesmy nods. Once. "Hurry up then."

I take the stairs in threes, leaping down and down again to the door. Inside, the floor is sticky, and the copper scent hits the back of my throat before I change to breathe through my mouth. I grab the bucket, full of scraps, fruit cores and old bread mostly, and tip it through the bars. The two remaining sailors huddle in the corner of the pen, eyes sunken, cheeks gaunt. I feel their gaze track me to the trough of scraps against the far wall. It lies directly under a small hole in the ceiling that runs from the kitchen. Whether my aunts chiselled the shaft themselves or found it there and built the kitchen and pens around it I've never been able to tell.

I dig the bucket into the trough, scooping out an extra helping, and pause as Menesmy's voice murmurs down the shaft.

"Where do you think she's going?"

Ligea snorts. "Unlike you to take an interest."

A faint tick-tick echoes down the hole: Menesmy's nails and needle working the loom. Then: "You don't smell it?"

"Of course I do! Everyday her stink grows stronger." I imagine Ligea's wrinkling her beak of a nose. "It's that wretched sea in her veins."

I stiffen at the edge of the trough. *Sea in my veins?* The bucket slips from my grasp and strikes the ground with a crack.

A pause from above. "So, can we eat her now?" Ligea asks, and I hear the crooked smile spreading her lips, revealing chiselled teeth. My mouth goes dry. They know I'm listening. I snatch the bucket, throw its slop through the bars and turn for the stair. Anger and fear vie for control. Sea in my veins. They knew. They'd always known. And there was only one way that could be. If the siren in me came from my mother, then the sea—

I burst into the kitchen, huffing from my ascent. Clear my throat. Ask the question I'd never dared to before.

"Who was he?"

Menesmy's fingers slow on the loom, but she keeps working. Needle darting in and out between the threads.

Ligea adjusts herself on her couch. "He's dead that's all you need know."

"I'm not leaving. You'll have to deal with my stink until you tell me."

"A sailor."

"A man with the sea in his heart," Menesmy says, so quiet I almost miss it.

Ligea grunts from her couch. "And his crotch. Swept your mother up and away with his charms he did. Then poisoned her. All to hatch a wretched snake." She spits the last word, eyes boring into me, accusing.

"Ligea," Menesmy warns from her loom. Too late. Because, suddenly, it all falls into place. All their anger. Ligea's hate. Menesmy's distance.

My mother didn't die at sea. She died for me. *Because* of me.

Menesmy's words come back to me. *Love is death.* Because love had created me, and it'd killed their sister. And looking at Ligea now, all that bitterness seething behind her gaze, perhaps Menesmy also meant death of a different kind.

And here I stand with the lineage of air and sea inside. Two worlds at odds. My tongue is thick in my mouth and it's all I can do to stop the gorge rising in my throat. "What did you do to him?" I ask, knowing and dreading the answer.

Ligea cackles. "We ate him of course!"

"Ligea!" Menesmy chides.

Ligea rounds on her sister, teeth clacking. "Why not tell her? Tell her how we cooked his meat until it fell off the bone. How we cracked him open and drank the marrow of our enemy. Tell her how it made us *strong*." Power licks her words, resonates in my head. "Strong enough that we could sing in a ship from *beyond* the horizon."

"Hush, Ligea," Menesmy squawks. She's risen from her loom. Beady eyes staring her sister down from across the table. "Say no more."

I stare at them, their lies unravelling like a loose thread on Menesmy's loom. "A witch never cursed you to stay," I say aloud. Eating a sailor of Poseidon's line—even if he was several times removed—would have angered the sea to no end. "Your own folly trapped you here."

Menesmy's long ago advice returns to me again. *Love is death, Fidi. You must never love.*

Why *that* lie?

Unless it was to keep me here. To stop me seeking more.

My chest constricts, like a hand has closed about my ribs and begun to squeeze. I take in their stooped shoulders, thinning white hair. Whatever power they'd gained, it was long faded. Age, time, maybe both to blame. That was why they kept me.

Power. They didn't just want to eat me. They wanted to crack me open and drink Poseidon's blood. And all this time they'd waited, circled, biding their time for the sea to take hold.

Now it had. And its power was growing; swelling into a fruit they'd pluck once it was ripe.

All this I realise in a heartbeat. And so do they.

I back up, feeling behind me for the start of the stair. "You monst—"

Ligea moves first. She lunges, long talons spreading wide, only to snatch at air as I twist away. I round the stair, make to flee.

"Stay where you are." Menesmy's song rocks through me. My legs turn heavy, as if I'm wading through mud. I hum under my breath, my husky notes unpicking Menesmey's spell. It sloughs away and I lurch up another step.

Then Ligea cracks the hearth's poker to the side of my head. The world tilts, dims, and crumples away.

I wake in the pens. The two sailors huddle in the furthest corner, like quail cornered by a fox in a coop.

Moving hurts. Breathing hurts. Even blinking. I'm not sure how long I lie there. A day, perhaps two, until my throbbing head subsides enough to attempt to rise. The moment I do, my stomach heaves and I retch onto the stone floor.

Not much comes up. Water, stomach acid, a trickle of blood from a wound reopened where I'd bitten my tongue. I shiver, curl into a ball and let the tide in my head take me back to darkness.

The second time I wake, my head is clearer. It still throbs, but when I move to put a hand to it, my vision doesn't spin. The blow from the poker has left a welt on one side of my head; a fiery length starting at the top of my cheek and stretching a thumb span past my left ear. My fingers probe the swollen flesh. No wetness, just crusted blood that leaves little red flakes on my hand as I rove it over the wound. Healing then, but I'll probably have headaches for weeks.

A temperature drop is the only sign that day has given way to night. I hug myself and eye the sailors. They're a miserable pair. Eyes distant, as if Charon has already claimed their souls and left these husks behind. Not one word passes between them.

By now, Caleus will wonder where I've gone. Probably worry too. My gut turns over. Enough to leave the safety of the beach? The thought pushes me to my feet and over to the cell door. Its hinges are rusted; it's been years since my aunts did any work on it. But when I shake it, the door holds.

Hades damn them. I spit on the floor, anger bubbling in my throat, threatening to overflow. I rest my head on the bars, wishing I could contort my body and slide through like my namesake. Breathe. Think. Think Fídi.

My traitorous mind stays blank.

Feet scuff on the stairs outside the pen. I turn my ear, two scuffs. Two sets of feet. Ligea *and* Menesmy. Together. Why? Menesmy's song resonates from the stairwell, notes high, cutting as a winter wind. My legs tremble, and without thinking it, one footsteps towards the door. *No, you don't.* I stamp and stuff my fingers in my ears before the song can claw more control away. Across the pen, the sailors shift, the first flicker of life I've seen in hours. They shake their heads, sway like sheep on a ship, and shuffle up to the bars.

My aunts sweep into view. Ligea grins at the sight of me, shameless as a child; wicked as a harpy. Menesmy looks bored.

I set my jaw and glare, and dig my fingers deeper.

"Stop resisting, little Fídi," Ligea coos. Her voice laps against Menesmy's, low and sultry, giving it a weight neither one has alone. My head spins. I shut my eyes, take a breath, open my mouth to sing my serpent song—then stop.

This was it. Risky. And only one chance. I swallow. If I don't succeed, I'll never leave this pen. Never see the sky. Never touch the sea again.

Never sing for Caleus.

I relax my hands, let them fall from my ears. *Trust your blood, Fídi. You are part siren too.*

Ligea and Menesmy's songs swirl into my head, snarling my thoughts like tangled rigging. Ligea's vibrato laughs in my ears. Menesmy approaches the door, draws out the key, undoes the lock. The bars swing open.

I stay the urge to lunge for the gap. Instead I'm meek, pathetic weak Fídi, whose power can't match that of her aunts'. Beside me, the sailors shuffle up to the door, file through. I struggle through my surprise. Both of them? Are they planning a multi-course feast? My breath catches.

I'm their sea-cursed dessert.

I suck in air, forcing my face still as my head swims in my aunts' song.

Please let this work.

I part my lips and hum. My voice is so faint, Ligea and Menesmy don't hear it. I concentrate on my own song. My snake's rasp and no one else's. Mine. Me. My head clears, my notes growing stronger in my mind, even as I keep my voice barely above a whisper. Ligea and Menesmy's melody pull my legs forward. Out I shuffle, behind the sailors. *Not yet.*

Ligea pulls out her knife.

I raise my voice, my song joining with my aunts' as I'd never dared do before. My rasp drives into my aunts' melody, sinks into it like fangs, chokes the harmony. The sailors blink. One twitches. The last hold on my muscles releases. A frown creases Menesmy's face.

The first sailor out of the pen, hair grey as a gull, gasps. I hiss one more note under my breath, pushing my will into the song. Not Ligea's, not Menesmy's, mine—my wish.

Fight. Live. Go free.

His face flushes, eyes ignite. He roars, drops his head, and barrels into Menesmy like a bull. She goes down with a screech. The second sailor wavers, head cocking to listen a little more. I turn my song on him. He stiffens, fist bunching as he rounds on Ligea. She dodges, skitters back from the stairwell.

"You!" she snarls at me. "This is your doing." Her talons reach for me, but I turn my voice louder, and cast off the last off the dregs of her power. I spin for the stairs. Flee. Get to Caleus and his raft. And pray to Poseidon it really is seaworthy.

"Come back, snake!" Ligea shrieks after me.

I block my ears and run.

He's stretched out beside the coals of a cold fire, sand sticking to his face.

Legs burning from running along the beach, I collapse at his side, grab both his shoulders and shake. "Caleus!"

His head wobbles once, snaps up. Dark eyes glint as he blinks. Recognition. A flash of a smile, then his forehead quivers. *Why are you here?*

"We've got to go," I hiss.

He squints, rubs his eyes and throws a log on the fire.

"No!" I kick sand over the light.

Another frown. *What are you-*

I place my hand on his cheek and turn his head so he can see my face, nose to nose with his in the dim. "Danger," I tell him. "*They're* coming."

He sucks in a breath, jaw tightening, fingers stiffening around mine. Then he's on his feet and pulling me towards the raft. We scurry around its bulk. He tests the ropes; I pile the last two amphorae onto the deck, hearing the slosh of wine in one. Caleus returns and lashes them to the planks, only to stop and sniff. He clucks his tongue, pulls the rope free of the cask of wine and rolls it off. *Not that one.* He breaks its cork seal and red sloshes over the terracotta lip like blood.

Empty, he thrusts it into my hands.

Water, he scrawls on the sand. *Cannot sail without it.*

Dread seeps into my stomach. The spring. It's not far from here. But it lies along a well-trod path, one my aunts will be scouring. I want to yell at him to forget the water and let us go. But Caleus knows the sea better than me. And I've seen what happens when creatures don't drink. They dry out, like fish scales in the sun. Then they die. If Caleus says we need it, we need it. I swallow and nod, leaving him to see to getting the raft onto the water.

It's a short trip along the worn goat track. I've walked it a thousand times, but I see my aunts in every shadow. Every ancient olive tree on the twisting path spurs my heart into my ribs, and each time I think, *this is it, this time it's them.*

They don't find me. When I reach the spring, I slump down at the shore and sink the amphora in. Its weight pulls on my grip as water glugs over the lip. My hands shake, palms clammy. *Calm down, Fidi.*

A screech stabs through the air. So high and loud it rattles my bones, sets my head throbbing. I sway, catching myself on the bank so as not to fall in.

The beach. It came from the beach. A strange fear surges inside me, submerging me in its tide. Cold frosts my gut, turns my breath short. Caleus.

I drop my amphora and sprint. Gods, please, no.

Down the track, past the twisted olives. Limestone cuts my feet; I barely feel it. A sob catches in my chest, I growl and force it down. *Tears won't help you, Fídi.* Onto the beach, across the sand, legs burning.

The cave is still when I reach it. Nothing moves. I slink inside, not daring to call out. A dim brightness shines from the fire: a single fresh log part burned through. *Damn it, Caleus, I said no light.* A shape lies on the other side of the flames. My knees turn weak, but I force my legs to cross the distance. One step, two.

The shape grows sharper, more distinct. Hope and horror douse me so fast I can't do anything but stare, unable to comprehend.

It's Menesmy.

She's dead.

A shaft of terracotta sticks from her throat. Blood flows thick from the wound, mixing with the wine in the sand. I shuffle closer, unable to stop my fingers from running over her silver hair, still as soft as down, even in death. Her eyes are open, mouth agape, confused shock etched forever on her face. Slowly, my mind puts it together.

My aunts had come looking for me, just as I'd known they would. Crossing the headland, their keen eyes would have spied the flicker of Caleus' fire from the clifftops. They'd found him here. Tried to work their magic over him. Only to realise too late that it didn't work.

And Menesmy had paid for that folly.

I can imagine Caleus' terror. It would have been as if the night had its claws into him. My stomach flutters as I study the sand: Menesmy's blood, no one else's. And unlike Menesmy, Ligea is quick on her feet. Which means—

"Oh Fídi," her song echoes from the headland. My muscles stiffen and a cool flush of strength rushes down my limbs. "Come Fídi, see what I have found."

She's perched on the edge of the cliff, heedless of the fall. Caleus hangs black and blue in her grip, head lolling. The sight throws me into a memory of Ligea throwing my doll into the fire. I'd clawed it out of the hearth, blistering my hands to save it. The toy had been irrevocably damaged, fire-snarled burns all over it and stained in charcoal. If anything, I'd loved it more. It had been flawed, like me.

"Let him go," I say.

Ligea's juts her chin, drags Caleus a step closer to the edge. "So *this* is what you were hiding."

I lurch forward. "No, don't!" the words slip out before I can think.

Ligea cackles. As if laughing with her, the sky rumbles in the distance. She clucks her tongue. "Love is death, or didn't you listen to dear Menesmy? It can crush your heart, little Fídi. Let me demonstrate."

Her fingers clamp around Caleus' throat. He twitches, gasps, and begins to gag. And before I can move, she swings him out over the edge of the cliff.

64

Caleus' eyes bulge at the drop. He grapples with Ligea's fingers, lashes out a kick. Then he looked to me, expression pleading, mouth shaping the word. *Fidi.*

The sea roars in my ears.

She releases him.

He plummets.

"No!" I'm running, charging, for what I don't know until I am a step from the cliff edge, and feel the sea calling below. I streak past Ligea, gather my strength, and leap.

"Idiot Fídi!" Ligea screeches. Her hands snatch after me: her precious little sea snake. She misses. And the ocean rises to meet me.

For a heartbeat, I dream again; hanging suspended in water, sand swirling under my toes. An urgency tickles my lungs, twinges at my collarbone. Air. Need air. I cough, a bubble breaks for the surface. Then I'm not dreaming.

I'm drowning.

Panic blinds me. I thrash, grab at the water like I'm climbing a tree, only to find no purchase. I sink lower.

Skin tingles.

Lungs burn.

Until I can't hold it in—or out?—anymore.

Open my mouth, suck the water in. Wait for it to choke my lungs; pray it will be quick.

But I don't choke. Instead, my lungs lighten, head clears as the blissful . . . air? water? rushes in. Whatever it is, I'm breathing it.

I run my hands along my throat, down my chest, marvelling. My fingers brush against ridges under my collarbone. I follow their shape: the skin is puckered like scars, and only when I feel them release a rush of water over my fingertips does it dawn on me.

Gills. *Poseidon be.*

A figure floats into my peripheral vision; face down above me. I blink and my vision sharpens in the gloom. Salt crusted hair swirls around a narrow face. Eyes shut, expressive brow lax. Caleus.

I dig at the water, scooping it like I might scoop sand. My body twists and I squirm through it like a worm. Gods damn it, I'm going nowhere. The sea might be in my veins, but I struggle like a hawk underwater. Caleus is dying and I can't reach him. I bite down a savage cry. *Swim, you sea-blooded snake. How hard can it be?*

An itch tingles over my hands, up my toes. I glance down. My toes are longer than I remember. Long and webbed—like a frog. I hold my hands up. My fingers too. Webbing grows between each digit.

Another dig at water again and my fingers fan open, pushing the water past. I ripple forward. *That's it.* I fix my sights on Caleus; kick my feet. I shoot forward, so fast I almost barrel into him. I grab his shoulders and pull him upwards. Something is happening to my legs, but I don't look. All I can think is, *don't be dead. Please don't be dead.*

Our heads break the surface.

Air gags my throat. I cough, gills spilling the water in my lung out. The next breath feels too light, lacking substance. But I draw in another, then another. I shake Caleus, slap his cheeks.

No response. Panic rises again. Heat burns at the corner of my eyes. Don't let this be how it ends. I shake him again, thump his chest. He coughs up water, but doesn't wake. My vision blurs. Ridiculous, why can't I see? It's just water isn't it?

"Wake up!" I scream and I throw my power behind the words. "Wake up Caleus!" The sea jumps, great concentric circles rippling away from me. Waves as tall as I am slam into the limestone cliff.

What in the gods—

A cackle echoes from above. "That's all you got?" Ligea stands on the ledge, beady eyes staring me down, laughing as I struggle. "Disappointing." She spits. "You can't save him. You can't even save yourself."

She lifts her hand and the clouds split. Light blinds, strikes the beach. The sound of it sends splinters through my ears. I shriek, diving my head below the water. The world above muffles. I release a breath, tighten my grip on Caleus.

You can't save him. I shove Ligea's taunts away. I must get him to shore. He can't stay out here like this. But Ligea is waiting. I grind my teeth. I can't hope to match her voice, but I can dampen it again—just as I did in the pens. *But first, let's see if this snake can sing underwater.*

I breathe in the sea, open my mouth, and sing.

The notes that come out are not mine—or not as I've known them. Gone is the rasping, wheezing voice. What comes is a melody that resonates within the water, as if the sea itself is singing. My power pulses through the blue, rising into white-peaked waves. I revel in it—was this inside me all along? Was this what my aunts wanted to devour?

Rage swells inside me. *How dare they.*

I unleash my rage, pounding the waves into the cliff. All their lies—*crash*—years of loneliness—*crash*—and, my chest squeezed, fear. *Crash.* So much fear. Fear that Caleus is beyond my help, that he will die, and it will be my fault. My last wave engulfs the rocks, sending spray high into the air.

The sea subsides and I float, power spent, fighting to keep Caleus' head above water.

Above, Ligea laughs, spits over the edge. "Is that all? Even with the sea you can't reach m—"

A crack sounds deep in the cliff. Pebbles bounce down to the sea, plop into the water. Fresh horror floods my limbs. It's coming down, the rock giving way. I throw an arm around Caleus and dive, kicking hard.

My legs move as one. Scales flash in the corner of my eye. Away. Get clear. We surge through the water with a speed I've never known—even on land. And for a heartbeat, I imagine this is what it is like to fly like a hawk. A hawk of the sea.

Behind, the cliff crumbles. A shrill, soprano scream sounds before its lost in the roar.

For a long minute, I bob on the surface, staring at the cliff and the smattering of new rock in the sea. Caleus' cave is gone. Menesmy gone. Ligea gone.

A groan in my arms.

"Caleus!" I shake him again. He coughs, eyes flutter open. Slowly, one hand touches his ear, then my mouth, and he smiles. *I heard you.*

I pull him close and laugh through my tears.

He steps onto the raft; I into the water. One last look back to the limestone cliffs and the twisted olives on the headland. Given time, I might come to miss this place. My mind returns to my aunts' cave, for the horror I'd been party to—and had aided. I shiver. I've not been back there. There's been no sighting of the last two sailors from the pens, though I've seen signs of their passing. Tracks from the spring, a trickle of smoke from a campfire on the next headland. I wish them luck, but have no desire to meet them again.

The sea pulls at my waist. Already the changes are starting. I hold my fingers up, watch the webbing spread.

A brush on my arm. Caleus leans from the raft, eyebrows questioning. *Are you ready?*

I nod. I'm not sure what lies ahead for us, but it's time to put this island at our backs. Caleus releases the raft's sail. It flops limp on the mast—trust him to pick a day without a breath of wind.

I sigh. "Need a tow?" I ask.

Caleus grins, taps his voice box, then mimes the music coming from my mouth. Suddenly, I'm sure our lack of wind is no mistake.

Sing me your song, sea daughter.

About the Author:

Nikky grew up as a barefoot 90s child in Perth, Western Australia, before moving to New Zealand in 2016. By day she works as a professional content writer and by night authors speculative fiction, often burning the candle at both ends to explore fantastic worlds, mine asteroids and meet wizards. Her creative work has appeared in magazines, on radio and in anthologies around the world. She is currently writing a dark fantasy trilogy, routinely sacrificing literary darlings to the editing gods in the hopes of seeing it published.

You can find her online at
W:nikkythewriter.com | T:@NikkyMLee | F:nikkythewriter

The Lighthouse Keeper

Stephen Herczeg

Every little town and fishing village that you encounter as you drive along the coast is as much like the one before as the one after. They sport the same style buildings, a similar beachfront, nowadays populated by little cafés and souvenir shops, a dock or pier, a small square with a memorial to the town's fallen soldiers, and of course an obligatory pub.

I've lived in Minnipa Bay all my life. We're a fishing community, but I never really sought a life at sea. I carried on from my father's business. A bit of carpentry and a lot of ship-wrighting among other jobs.

My old Dad always said, "It's better to keep 'em afloat than float around in 'em."

He was right. It's rare to drown on dry land, but we've lost a lot of sailors to the ocean over the years. The sea is a harsh mistress.

Those losses have given belief to a lot of legends. Stories of sailors drowned, of ships lost, even of ghost ships found.

No other legend has grown in stature down through the years than the story of the *Peligrande*. Almost two decades ago, a large container vessel ran aground on the rocks below the lighthouse. It was in all the local and national papers at the time, but as the years wore on the knowledge of that night has been lost.

Except to the people of Minnipa Bay, and especially to the one man who was closest to the action on that night, Old Jack, the former lighthouse keeper, retired ever since that night.

Old Jack is the one who has kept the legend alive the most, each and every night he can be found in the same chair in the bar of our local pub.

As I sat on my normal stool at the bar, he prepared to repeat the same story I've heard hundreds of times.

"Been lighthouse keeper for nigh on fifty years and I ain't seen nothin' so strange as that night," Old Jack said, drinking deep from his beer.

Sometimes he would repeat the story to himself or those of us nearby, but during the weekends and summer months he could find a new set of ears to entrance.

The majority of his audience were tourists that had found their way into the pub looking for a bit of seaside charm. One look at

Old Jack's grizzled features and they could be convinced to buy him a beer in exchange for a rare tale of the sea.

Old Jack took another draw from his beer and put down the empty glass. He eyed the man to his left, who indicated to the barkeep for another. Jack had his quarry well in his sights. Tonight's audience were well into their fifties and looked like a pair of newly minted grey nomads, touring the coastal towns and villages to gain as much exposure to the citizens and atmosphere as they could. Bumping into an old salt like Jack would be almost a holy grail sized prize in their eyes.

Once the full beer was placed down before Jack, he continued. "The night came in dark much quicker than regular," he said, "they that tell us the weather said there was a great storm a brewin' down in the south and a heading towards us."

I remember that night as if it was just last night.

It was before Dad left us. We'd been working on fixing a deep crack in a small fishing boat's hull down at the dry dock when the radio told us that a storm was coming north and suggested we secure all loose items and get indoors.

Big squalls weren't rare, but they seldom made landfall, and as I looked out across the grey ocean I saw the dark, thick clouds on the horizon closing in on us. Within moments they'd turned the late afternoon into deep night.

The wind whipped up and the sea sent great, foaming waves crashing against the shore and deep into our little bay. The fishing boats in the harbour rocked furiously with each new assault.

We strapped down the boat we were working on and I glanced towards the lighthouse.

Even from where I stood, massive waves smashed the rocks at its base. The old man had been diligent. The light shone brightly, but couldn't penetrate far into the thick, low-hanging cloud. The mournful sound of a foghorn cut through the darkness, but in the end it wasn't enough.

Growing up in Minnipa Bay I'd survived through storms all my life, but this one was different. It wasn't just wind and rain; it was almost as if there was a malevolence behind it. I know I'm just attributing some level of intelligence to an act of nature, but this was no ordinary storm.

That night I lay awake listening to the storm as it lashed the village. The fear that the howling wind would rip the sheets of galvanised iron from our roof drove me under my covers, at least that what I tell myself now, but at the time I was more afraid of what lurked within the tempest itself. When I had been almost lulled asleep by the wind and waves, the tone of the foghorn changed. The sound became more urgent, repeating in short sharp bursts instead of the long lowing tone.

And then I heard it.

A great grinding shriek as metal met rock. It echoed out over the storm and tore strips down my mind, like fingernails down a blackboard.

Within moments I had thrown on some clothes, grabbed a rain slicker and was fighting my way across the village through the blasting rain. Giving no thought to my father, some inner sense drove me on towards the emergency on the shore.

I reached the edge of the tiny promontory that led out into the broiling waves. The lighthouse was a dark tower topped by the revolving light that shone meekly into the darkness.

A crack of lightning showed me the devastation on the rocks at the base of the lighthouse.

A massive container ship had run aground. I would find out later that it was the *Peligrande*, a ship that operated out of Lisbon in Portugal. She had travelled far across the wide seas to find her death on the rocks of this desolate coastline.

I could discern no lights aboard the enormous vessel. I thought that the Captain was either blind to the dangers of this coastline or worse.

It turned out the reality was a sorrier tale than I imagined.

I took a sip of my own beer and turned my attention to Old Jack telling his version. He was the one who knew the story best.

"I was afeared that night. The storm was the worst I'd ever seen in me long life. I dint think there'd be any ships within sight of my lamp. I'd checked the charts and there were none due, but a storm's a storm, and Captains is only human. I stood up on the gantry below the lamp and stared out at the black night. The lightning blasted the darkness, the thunder cracked as if breaking the Earth apart. Then I sees it. A great white hulk was spearing straight for shore. I rushed downstairs and honked the foghorn trying to get their attention. I looked out me little porthole to spy the ship and saw it was almost on me."

He took a sip, leaving his audience on the edge of their seat for a moment before continuing.

"I started down the stairs. It's a long way down that tower but I knew I had to get out of there. Halfway down I hears it. A sound no seaman or keeper ever wants to hear. Metal scraping across the jagged rocks. I stopped near a window and looks out. There I saw the great ship's last gasp as it ground up onto the rocks below. I watch it come to a stop. Stupid idjit Captain, I thinks to meself as I makes me way down the stairs."

He shuffles around in his seat, partly as a pause, partly to relieve the tension on his buttocks.

"I comes out and sees that giant hulk with its bow crushed against the rocks. No lights on. Nothing. I looks up at the deck. No movement. Nothing. A flash of lightning shows me the hand holds cut into her side. I'm old, but I forgets all that and climbs up onto the deck. I expected there to be people running around like headless chickens, but I dint see nobody. The only thing I sees that's out of the ordinary are these strange scratches on the rail and deck. I ignores them and heads towards the bridge. The ship was fully loaded, there's containers stacked up almost as high as the lighthouse. She was a biggun, I tells you that. I sees more of them scratches but can't make out too much. Up the stern gangway I go and enters the bridge, just as a flash of lightning lights up the sky behind me. Then I sees what's inside the bridge."

Jack takes another sip of beer, draining the glass which is quickly replaced by another filled to the brim. He nods in thanks and begins again.

"There's blood. Everywhere. Splashed all over the cabin, and more of those scratches. I peers around, but there's no bodies. Nothing. I almost screams when the thunder cracks. Me hearts a thumping, but I backs out of that carnal house. It's time to leave this to the authorities, I thinks and steps out on to the deck. I climb down the gangway and start to head back to the bow. Another crack of lightning and then I sees it. As tall as a man, carrying a load on its shoulders. It sidles up to the railing and tosses something over the side. It stands up straight, notices me and turns my way. I think it's a man, maybe a pirate robbing the ship."

Jack stopped and took another sip, letting the story and his audience hang on every word.

"A bolt of lightning cracks the sky. I sees it in all its glory. Eight feet high. Black-green scaly skin. Great clawed hands with webbing 'tween the fingers. Eyes like huge black pits. A mouth full of needles for teeth. A face from hell. Over its shoulder it carried a blood-soaked man. Dead, I reckons. That thing was taking him to the deep to feed on. The night went dark again and by the time another bolt hit, it was gone."

"I hurried off that doomed ship as fast as my legs could carry me. I've never seen anything like that thing before, but I'll remember that horrible face until the day I die."

Old Jack always finished by downing the last of his beer and holding out hope for another. Very rarely does his glass remain empty.

About the Author:

Stephen is an IT Geek, writer, actor, film maker and Taekwondo Black Belt based in Canberra Australia. He has been writing for over twenty years and has completed a couple of dodgy novels, sixteen feature length screenplays and dozens of short stories and scripts.

Stephen's scripts, TITAN, Dark are the Woods, Control *and* Death Spores *have found success in international screenwriting competitions with a win, two runner-up and two top ten finishes.*

His horror stories have featured in various anthologies including: Sproutlings; Hells Bells; Trickster's Treats #1, #2 and #3; Shades of Santa; Below the Stairs; Behind the Mask; Beyond the Infinite; Beside the Seaside; The Body Horror Book; Anemone Enemy; Petrified Punks; Beginnings; Sea of Secrets, Demonic Carnival; Deep Space; A Tribute to H.G. Wells; What If?; Through Death's Door and Coffins and Dragons.

Over forty of his drabbles have been accepted by Blood Song Books; Black Hare Press; Fantasia Divinity and ThingsInTheWell.

You can catch Stephen at his Facebook page:
https://www.facebook.com/stephenherczegauthor

OLYMPUS9

Tee Linden

Gany steals a moment in the cool and clear-walled thoroughfare of Earth-orbiting Olympus9. One hand holds the water jug, his other palm presses against the invisible barrier. Earth turns beneath his feet as Gany listens to himself breathe. From here, Gany can hold watch over seas, cloud whorls and vast, sunburnt deserts. And he can claim witness to all the invisible people living on the surface in their billions.

He is one of them. He was. But a lucky one, according to his mother. He was one that escaped the slums. Escaped wasting diseases that spread as easily as scrub fire, from the familiar hunger that settled down at night with you, in the plundered vast and dusty sprawl. The Company locks its cities tight. The slums outside grow grateful labourers, like firm, ripe oranges from armed and gated Company farms, grown with Company-owned and diverted rivers.

Gany closes his eyes and breathes deeply. The air is recirculated, reverse-scrubbed through carbon and scented with pine, but there is always a stale thread to it. It never smells quite right.

When Gany left the slums—one of the select few to make it into the Company—his head was filled with possibility. With change. He believed his life was unfolding, ready for what would come, ready for the sunrise to peek up behind the glow of the Earth.

But he learned. He feels he is aging fast on Olympus9. His mind and self growing too fast and big for the walls that contain him. These days, when he reaches end cycle and retires to the cramped crew quarters with his joints aching, he dreams of changing again. Of red feathers sprouting itchy-wet from his sunless flesh.

All he wanted was out. Everyone wanted out. Wanted more than sickness and dying and scratching a living from patches of parched soil. But getting out took money and only the Company had that.

He wanted to change and the Company ships seemed ethereal from the slums, hanging in the heavens. He wanted a new life. One without boundaries. He sold his debts to them, a sacrifice to the gods of potential dreams, but it was all just smoke and mirrors. Gany found himself in a beautiful cage. If escaping the slums was difficult, escaping Olympus9 is impossible. There is nowhere to go. No way to leave. No doors. No outside.

So he pauses in the walkway as he always does. He takes Company-time like a thief. He breathes their air. Enjoys the mirror shine of polished glass and he embraces the view that wasn't designed for him. He absorbs it. The Earth seems boundless.

Gany's too-thin uniform prickles against his skin as he watches Earth through his wide-eyed reflection. The window is luxurious, like nothing in crew quarters. He doesn't belong up here. He is only allowed here because he brings water to the people who do belong. Sons of kings. Owners of spaceports and asteroid mines. Supreme leaders hovering far above the mere mortals sick and scratching in the dirt below. Important Company men discussing important things. You have to be important to belong on Olympus9. Too important to fetch your own water. Someone must bring it to you.

Gany will never be the man who has water brought to him. He scratches phantom itches as he imagines his life ticking out in servitude and his gaze flees to the stars. All the beyond.

The door at the end of the hall opens. Laughter spills out. His supervisor, weathered to a sunless grey, frowns at Gany loitering. Gany obediently brings the water jug, abandoning his watch.

There is a small window in the crowded crew quarters and it looks into the stars. Gany sits next to it on an upturned box, reaching beneath his thin uniform to scratch the now persistent itching on his lower back.

This end cycle could be a hundred other end cycles. Everything bleeds into an ever-running loop on Olympus9. Every moment plays out like the ones before, the ones to come. They are fed flavourless nutrition blocks and they shower and they ready themselves for the next cycle. It smells like bodies down here, of lasting sweat, of skin and hair. A smell Gany remembers from the slums, the smell humans have when they live on top of each other. As usual, he watches beautiful nothing as the other crew members joke and play cards and settle down for sleep.

They are from the slums like him. Everyone in the crew quarters is young, like him, and attractive. He notes this is the Company preference for those plucked from the slums and is reminded again of oranges on the Company-run farms. As a child he and boys from the slums once risked the guards and sneaked into a Company farm near home. They clawed into firm stolen fruit, the flesh bright and sweet on their tongues, juice sticky as it ran between their fingers. Perfect oranges are kept by the Company for the staff, and any scarred, bruised or almost rotten fruit is relinquished to the churning slums. Gany assumes this end awaits him as well. He will eventually be returned to the slums; scarred, bruised or almost rotten.

That persistent itch returns and his fingers come scratching up beneath his white shirt, across his lower back. His flesh is hot from his scratching and when he pulls his hand away he finds crescents of blood beneath his trimmed nails. The blood is bright as poppies. As red as the feathers in his dreams.

Down in the slums on Earth, Gany's mother used to tell him bedtime stories of red-feathered spectrals. They were made from travellers lost from broken ships or faulty docks, floating through the void, destined to a lonely, mad death when their oxygen depleted. Like his father, a Company asteroid miner in a badly-maintained ship, who was sucked out into space and disappeared.

Spectrals change those lost ones. Smiled upon by some ancient and gracious god, weak human skin bleeds feathery. They become bright as dying stars, shining creatures that soar through space. Wrapped up and changed by the cosmic dust of creation.

And they could be anyone. All are equal on the altar of the void. Untethered.

The stories were popular in the slums. They were created to quell crying children, to explain absences of parents or siblings lost in space, no body to return to the dust. They were stories of bristling hope. A heaven above heavens. A way to look up from the dry wastes and find those lost among the stars, never returning. It was a better end than a frozen body cartwheeling into eternity, on a path lit by stars never reached by the Company.

Gany looks out the window, calculating how far a body might travel if it were sucked out into the vacuum of space. He assumes his father would still be travelling as fast now as he was when the ship cracked. Too far to ever catch up with. Too far to ever find. A frozen human meteorite venturing to other nebulas.

A crewmate taps Gany on the shoulder, gesturing at his back. Gany twists on his crate, peering at what he can see of his lower back. Blood blooms through the cheap white uniform. Gany sighs and pulls it off, inspecting the damage.

He has to get this to the laundry. He can't wear a stained uniform. The Company wouldn't allow that imperfection from him.

Gany is in the cool and clear-walled thoroughfare of Earth-orbiting Olympus9 with a water jug. Again. As before. As in the future. His uniform is bleached and as pristine as the hallway. He refuses to scratch his back though the material feels like sandpaper against his itching skin. He steals time from the Company, dawdling, soaking in the beauty of Earth. He floats above it. The Earth expands before him. He imagines he is a spectral, and he is watching over Earth with eyes made from the dust of ancient planets, he is created anew, feathered and untethered.

If he could, he would watch over the seas, cloud whorls and vast sunburnt deserts until the Company cities crumbled. Until the slums were flooded and became verdant and boundless. He would soar above it. He would hunger for nothing and he would answer to no one.

Gany knows it's just a story told to children, but he can't help but hold onto the thought of becoming something else. It's a guiding star. Maybe that's why he debt-sold himself out here. Trying to find something. He's as lost as ever.

He winces against the scratchiness that burns in his back.

His stolen moments never last long. He is somehow needed and ignored all at once. The lords of Olympus9 need water. That's his purpose, to bring it to them and to stand silently by until more is needed. There is something comforting in the idea that as much power as they wield, making life and death decisions that trickle down to the world far below, Company men need water just as much as Gany. They are not gods. They are only men.

The door at the end of the hall opens and arguing voices spill out. Gany can smell the bright citrusy tang of oranges. The fragrance catches in his nose, slicing brilliant through the dull recirc air. He is a child again, stealing the forbidden fruit, sticky juice between his fingers. Within the room of men, a glass sculpture sits grand upon a table, twisting and reaching like roots. Oranges, whole and severed, decorate the sculpture. Firm and fresh fruit made wastefully ornamental. The oranges, sweet-scented and bright, are untouched.

Resentment bubbles up in Gany, thick and hot. A sick sweat breaks out across him, can feel it sprout over his upper lip. His head is filled with the scent and the waste of the fruit-filled extravagant sculpture.

Gany's supervisor—still weathered and sunless—appears at the door, blocking the sculpture. He shakes his grey-streaked head at Gany and gestures for him to come.

Gany's back itches, and the itch is spreading, like fire caught on the wind, spreading to dry twigs and crunchy leaves. His body is rebelling. Against the order. Against his obedience. Against existing in Olympus9.

Gany's sick and sweating palm smears perspiration across the perfect surface. A sudden sting in his lower back makes his body jerk—puppet like—and water splashes out of the jug, soaking his uniform. He drops the jug and it rolls away, spilling water in decaying circles.

Gany is aware that his supervisor is complaining, but his words are meaningless. Gany's body is hot enough that the water soaking his uniform is evaporating in clouds of escaping steam. He reaches up under the thin uniform to the swathe of skin at the centre of the galaxy. His fingers track the desert of his back, finding a tiny thorn protruding, sharp and bloody from his back. He twists, mad and panting, looking at the reflection of his body imprinted over the Earth, trying to see what's stuck in him. A tiny thing beneath the pad of his fingers. Tiny, stubborn and full of fire. He pinches it between his nails and feels the comforting release of the irritant sliding from his flesh, a feeling so intense he groans as it pulls free.

He holds it up before his face, between him and the Earth. He breathes heavy. Between his thumb and forefinger he holds a wet, red feather, plucked fresh and vibrant from his skin.

About the Author:

Tee Linden is a writer living south of Sydney. She loves writing SFF, especially if it involves the Australian bush. You can find her tweeting under @tearannosaurus or her website is teelinden.com

Where Are Your Sheep?

Frank Prem

Ganymede

Ganymede

where are your sheep

gone

dear boy

was it not

you

who was the one

meant to keep them

safe from harm

yes it was

but the eagle came

I saw

from the stars above

to claim you

Zeus is god

and you

are just a toy

a plaything

for his pleasure

for a while

carry water

run

his bath

carry water

WHERE ARE YOUR SHEEP?

bathe
his feet

fetch for him
and carry
young Aquarius

but
while you drift
all around the sky
with your pitcher
your pail

the sheep
that were your chore
have wandered

curse you
fell god

I curse you
old Jove

oh

Ganymede

my Ganymede

your sheep

are

all of them

gone

About the Author:

Frank Prem has been a storytelling poet for forty years. When not writing or reading his poetry to an audience, he fills his time by working as a psychiatric nurse.

He has been published in magazines, e-zines and anthologies, in Australia and in a number of other countries, and has both performed and recorded his work as 'spoken word'.

Frank has published three collections of free verse poetry – Small Town Kid *(2018),* Devil In The Wind *(2019), and* The New Asylum *(2019).*

He and his wife live in the beautiful township of Beechworth in northeast Victoria (Australia).

Author Page (Newsletter sign up): https://FrankPrem.com
Facebook page: https://www.facebook.com/frankprem2
Twitter: @frank_prem

Skewed Futures

Fallacious Rose

This week, those born under the sign of the Water Carrier can expect . . .

Jemima took a sip of coffee and pushed herself a little out of her seat so that she could check Eliza's office. Behind the glass wall, Eliza sat half-obscured behind her own computer screen. She didn't lift her eyes: her cheeks were drawn inwards towards her mouth in that expression some people have when they're completely absorbed and not altogether happy. Manager stuff.

Returning to her screen, Jemima arranged her own face in lines of studious concentration, and scrolled down.

With Uranus in the house of Pluto, now may be a good time to take another look at your financial affairs. For those Aquarians in a relationship . . .

She hit the scroll bar again. At the age of thirty-one, she was not in a relationship, and hadn't been for three years.

. . . while for those who are single, love may be on the horizon . . . READ MORE

Jemima rarely bothered to click the *Read More* button: there were always other pages to visit, celebrity click-bait to bite. But today—depressed by a weekend spent mainly alone with her collection of stuffed toys—she moved the mouse over the text to reveal the rest of the article. She didn't believe in horoscopes; still, they cheered her up with their vague optimism. Unlike her elder sister Ruby, who said Jemima would never find a man if she didn't at least clean her bathroom properly.

. . . on the romance front, today you will meet a tall, dark and handsome man. You will develop an instant crush, but I'm afraid he won't be at all interested in you. He's married, so that's just as well. Later you'll go home and have three gin and tonics and a family sized chocolate bar, then you'll call your ex-boyfriend, Max. He won't be interested either.

What? Jemima blinked, and brought her face closer to the screen, as if somehow the letters might re-arrange themselves into normality if she just squinted hard enough at them.

And on the career front, your boss will catch you looking up your horoscope in work time and will call you in for a 'counselling' session. Since this is the third time she's had to speak to you about your performance, she will make veiled threats about your future with the company and you will start to cry . . .

"Jemima! Will you come into my office, please?"

Jemima had been so absorbed—transfixed—that she hadn't even noticed Eliza padding out of her office in her stockinged feet, creeping up right behind her. She jumped and almost swore.

"I'm just . . ."

"So I see."

She followed Eliza glumly into her office. *I won't cry, anyway.* But as soon as Eliza brought up the fact that she was, after all, on three months' probation, and suggested that she should look around for some more suitable employment, Jemima felt her eyes stinging and her face turning hot. She hated being told off.

She went back to her desk, conscious of the covert glances following her—pity, curiosity, schadenfreude. It was this job—he didn't seem to be able to do anything right. They hadn't prepared her at university for this—this drudgery. And why did it matter so much if 'it's' had an apostrophe or not, or how many verbs there should be in a sentence?

She sat down, her lip trembling, and opened a file. Suddenly it struck her with the force of a slap—the horoscope had been right. Those words, then—they must have been written for her, and only her. Somehow, Lorelei Stargazer had seen through the mists of the future, her future, and stuck it up on the net for all to see—but no, how could that be? How could Lorelei know what was happening to a total stranger, in an anonymous office, right then?

It's a hack, thought Jemima. Someone's hacked my account, somehow, and put that stuff up there. That doesn't make sense, she answered herself. *Lots of people look at Lorelei's horoscopes, not just me.* But this gave rise to a further horrible thought: *how many people are looking at this right now? How many people are laughing and sharing and commenting on this pathetic person, Jemima Clarke, a failure in love and at work?*

She ached to flick back over to the horoscope page, to assure herself that she hadn't been hallucinating, but with Eliza's sharp glances through the glass and Olive, the Assistant Director, at the desk right behind her, she didn't dare. Still, as soon as the digital display read twelve noon, she almost ran to the lift, hopped her way from one foot to the other until it reached the ground floor, and then hurried outside. Once in the street, she called up her sister, Ruby.

"You'll never guess what happened to me!"

" *You?* Have you seen the news? The internet's gone crazy!"

"Wha—what?"

"Apparently all these people—all Aquarians—have got these personalised horoscopes and they're like, true. I mean, right down to what they were going to eat for lunch."

"But . . . but . . ."

"Unbelievable. Everywhere. Even in Pakistan—they don't even have star signs in Pakistan! Can you believe that?"

"Uh . . . yeah, actually." Jemima told her what had happened. "You think I was hacked or something?"

"What, you and everyone else born in February? I don't think so Midget." Ruby liked to remind Jemima how much shorter she was than her sister. And fatter.

"Shit." Jemima's mind boggled. "You mean someone, somehow, *knows* . . . the future?"

"Maybe they're kind of like, hypnotising everyone. Did you see any wavy lines or anything? Or . . . maybe it's the government. You know they can watch you through your webcam now . . ."

"Or it could be—do you think astrology's true? I mean really true? Maybe it's just—maybe Lorelei's the real thing, maybe she really can see into the future."

"Yeah maybe. Wonder if she can see if you're ever going to get a life, what do you think, Midget? That'd be worth knowing."

"Shut up—and don't call me that."

Jemima spent the next hour pretending to focus on a memo she was supposed to be drafting. Her stomach churned its own rhythm of fear and confusion. She felt as if the entire building had turned inward to stare at her, as if every keystroke confirmed some destiny defined but not controlled, not by her. Nauseous, she rushed to the toilet, and once in the cubicle, sat numb and motionless. If she didn't move, she somehow felt instinctively, *they* couldn't see her.

At last she had to come out, and found that the whole office was clustered around a colleague's computer.

"Only Aquarians?" Jack the admin assistant was saying disappointedly. "Why not Libra?" Jack was a typical Libra: he'd believe anything.

"Or Capricorn. Don't tell me you believe this star sign shit?" said Olive. Like most Capricorns, she was down to earth and had a tendency to be trenchantly sceptical.

"What are you all standing about for?" Eliza trotted out of her office. This time she had her pumps on.

"It's this horoscope thing," said Olive. "Apparently, horoscope sites around the world are telling everyone exactly what's going to happen to them. Exactly, But it's just Aquarians, for some reason. I don't see what's so special about them."

"Aquarians *are* special. That's the whole thing about being an Aquarian, they're different, free spirits. And it's the Age of Aquarius, isn't it?" said Jack.

Olive snorted, while Eliza shook her head in despair at the foolishness of mankind.

"Sounds like fake news to me."

"Well, you're Aquarian, why don't you go look? Just google 'Aquarius horoscope'," said Anna, the team's social media expert. She and Eliza went to lunch together; she could afford to be bossy with her.

They all watched Eliza stalk back to her office and scowl at her own screen, as if willing it to defy her. Her face froze. She rose, and shut the door.

That night, Jemima drank three gin and tonics and ate a family sized chocolate bar. She needed it. Then, drunk, she phoned Max, and poured out her near-hysteria into the invisible ear. Max hung up.

The next day, she woke late and hurried for the bus. As soon as she had a seat she pulled out her iPhone and googled 'Aquarius horoscope'. The page results were clogged with headlines: 'Horoscope Horror', 'Big Brother is Watching You Right Now' and 'Astrology Not Crap After All'—but she flicked past those impatiently, and on to Lorelei's advice for the day.

Today, Aquarian ladies should watch out for . . .

Someone slid into the seat next to her, looked across at the screen, and smirked.

"Weird, isn't it?"

He was dark, and handsome. Probably tall as well, judging by the legs. But wasn't this supposed to have happened yesterday, Jemima wondered?

"Uh . . . yeah." Maybe things were looking up. She remembered that horoscopes, as a rule, ended on a positive note.

"You an Aquarian?"

"Can't you tell by the shoes," she quipped, suddenly witty. She'd read that you could always tell an Aquarian by the way their shoes didn't match their outfit. Hers were green Doc Martens, worn with a Kmart standard issue black office skirt.

He looked bemused. "Uh, yeah, I guess. Anyway, d'you think it's for real?"

The bus stopped. Blurred shapes got on and off. She was only aware of eyes as luxuriously liquid as Dutch chocolate, a hint of Blue Ocean aftershave.

"I don't know." She tore herself away, bent towards the phone.

Today, you will encounter a tall dark stranger. He will turn out to be a Gemini, which just happens to be your perfect match . . .

"I'm a Gemini," said the man, his thigh pressing against her own.

. . . and like all Geminis, although he's extremely charming, he's also a bit of a playboy. You're the first woman he's chatted up today, but there will be three more—one at the water cooler in his office, and the other two at the retirement celebration he's going to attend at a city bar after work . . .

"Is all this true?"

The man leaned in towards her, his cheek almost grazing hers as he read.

"Well . . ."

"It is, isn't it?"

A short silence filled the space between them. Someone in one of the seats behind said, "I've always been a believer, you know."

"I could always change," he said, softly and with a deft touch of serious. "For instance, I could decide not to go to that retirement party . . ."

"Yes, but you can't just decide. It says here . . ."

"No it doesn't," he said, lifting the phone from her hand and pointing with an index finger. "Look."

She read.

Like all Geminis, he can be a flirt, but when he meets the girl of his dreams, all that goes out the window—this man will be utterly faithful to you. Today, he will ask you out to dinner and you will say yes. It will be the beginning of a great romance. For you, things are only going to get better.

She felt a weight lift from her heart.

"So are you going to ask me out for dinner, then?"

"Dinner? But we only just met. And this is my stop."

She watched in disappointment as he got off, waving a casual hand in farewell. She looked down at the screen. Of course, the words had changed. Again. So it wasn't a prediction at all—just some kind of sick real-time recording of her life. Someone being funny. Probably God. She felt like throwing the phone out the window. But didn't.

Instead, she scrolled to the very end of the article and saw there, in the kind of italics that insurance documents use to tell you that you are not covered for fire if it involves any actual flames.

Disclaimer: All predictions above are subject to the observer effect, ie, the theory that simply observing a situation or phenomenon necessarily changes that phenomenon. No liability for deviations from the predicted future will be assumed by this astrologer.

About the Author:

I live on a rural property on the south-east coast of NSW, Australia, and write under the pen name Fallacious Rose. My elder sister reckons nobody will take me seriously with a name like that but then, I'm not sure I want them to—at least, not always. My brand is 'eccentric', my genre is 'everything', and the only thing standing between me and a career as a famous singer is . . . that I can't really sing. You can find out more, and download a story or two, at www.fallaciousrose.com.

BRAIN TRUST

Dorian Morrow

The Feeder hadn't slept for months. Not properly, anyway. Instead, he spent his days stooped in the armchair of his apartment, staring drearily at the view of shingled rooftops and horizon beyond his Smart Window. Each day, neither awake nor asleep he waited for the boiling orange orb in the sky to melt into the horizon. Images of the weather forecasts and cute cat videos cut into the sky like misshaped, man-made clouds. Beyond the glass projections, the sky flickered undecidedly between the radiant blue day and the empty night sky.

The news anchor's face replaced the sun, "The Brain Trust has informed us that GHOTI is predicting with ninety-seven percent accuracy, that unseasonably dry weather and resulting droughts will occur throughout the food production regions over the next three years. The Brain Trust has assured us that a solution to this problem will be found within the hour. Have faith in GHOTI Brain Trust."

The sky, scattered and pixelated, leaped between day and night in rapid spasms again.

The Feeder, still wearing his white overalls with their happy red and yellow GHOTI embroidered logo, sighed and walked over to the window. He thumped it twice with the palm of his hand. The sky fluttered momentarily and corrected itself to the sunset he'd been admiring moments earlier. The screen was working again, but the flickering images continued to flash deep within his head. Clamping his eyes shut was all he could do to maintain his balance.

The dreams were what kept him up all day. The dreams of work. It was a hellish cycle to be trapped in. To slave all night and then dream of it all day was beyond cruel. Each evening, when he clocked in to work, his mind was always fuzzy. He made mistakes which he had to fix before anyone noticed. He was always behind in his work, and by the end of his shift, when his head hit the pillow—instead of escape—his dreams created an itinerary of all the things he needed to do the next day.

But for now, all that he could do was focus on existing.

The Feeder rushed through the narrow cobblestone streets, lined with high apartments stacked above shop fronts; all constructed with centuries old stones that once fit together one way or another in a civilisation now dismantled and long forgotten. The bustling cities all over the world, built upon the graveyards of glass and concrete that once dominated the landscapes at the end of the twenty-first century, all shared this quaint, ivy lined façade. It was a neon-clad renaissance. An electric paradise of steepled rooftops that sloped comfortingly over the little artisan bakeries and delicatessens that had replaced those megamalls the Feeder learned about in school.

The city was coming to life, people laughed and sipped wine as they danced merrily from restaurant to bar, from bar to party. These creatures, revelling in a perpetual childhood, were, to the Feeder, strangers living strange existences. To him, their laughter and never-ending cycle of happiness provided by the Trust, was no more than an abstract memory, crumbling like the history of the Old World.

The Feeder took a turn onto Nike lane and crossed Coke bridge. As the laughter and sounds of music faded into the distance, he turned onto the iPath.

When did I lose connection? He pondered. He blamed his neurotic contemplations on the insomnia and concerned himself with the long-term damage the sleep deprivation was causing his brain. *It had to be more than the stress of work*, he thought. He retraced his memory in search for the roots of his sleepless nights, but his inability to grip any true memory only increased his anxiety.

The GHOTI Brain Trust building, a featureless black box occupying a cubic kilometre, eclipsed the night sky. The House that ruled the world.

In desperation, he searched his mind for childhood memories—anything that could assure him that he existed—but all of them were eroded by time, weathered and worn to shapes so generic they could be experiences that belonged to characters he saw on the Window. The nostalgia of his father teaching him to ride a bike. A fond memory he always held close. He tried to recapture every distinct detail. The way his father's strong hands would balance the seat whenever the bicycle began to wobble. But no matter how hard he tried to picture it, his father's face had dissolved from his memory like a sun-bleached photograph.

All that remained of his mother were the echoes of her voice, scolding him for playing with matches. The only memory left of his childhood friend was a nameless boy, ten or so, who fell out of a tree. Even then, the memory was just a feeling. The sadness he felt listening to the boy's tears. The guilt and shame he felt for the helpless ants he scorched with a magnifying glass. All the memories that made him who he was, and steered his actions for all these years had now faded. What stood in their place was the sinking feeling that a part of him was missing and could not be retrieved.

Out the front of the Brain Trust building, surrounded by candles and their LED picket signs, the protestors woke from their dreary slumber as he approached. Each day this group were waiting for him. The Committee for Free Market Enterprise. The lowly corporation owners, who spat at him, and screamed in his face as if he were the one making the decisions. Their digital signs flashed frowning faces and colourful phrases like *"We deserve our profits"*, *"Brain Trust must go!"* and *"GHOTI = dictatorship"*. These throwbacks of an archaic time, descendants of once mighty empires now stripped of their powers, the one percent who would rather blame this *nobody* Feeder for their classless utopia, than go out and enjoy it. The Feeder lowered his dark face and pushed through their words.

He considered joining them. Giving up. But it wasn't that easy. He was one of the few people left who still chose to work. Moreover, he had the honour of being one of last two *actual* people still employed by a global government that had automated all but ninety-nine percent of its operations. But what kept him working there wasn't the honour, but rather the twelve people he was responsible for keeping alive.

If they could be regarded as people, that is.

He toiled, despite his restless nights and dissolving recollections, because of the part he played. However insignificant, he was a cog in the machine that made everything else in this world possible. The innate predisposition to be a better person had left a pit inside him that could only be filled with the desire to isolate himself. A need to disconnect despite feeding the loneliness and solitude from which he felt no escape.

He passed through the security doors and into the halls of the city-sized computer. The main lobby was filled with artefacts of the Old World and the soothing, faceless voice of GHOTI narrating its existence on a recorded loop.

"Welcome back, Feeder." The warm voice was everything he wished his mother's was.

"GHOTI is an artificial intelligence entrusted by the people, to govern the people, for the people. The Brain Trust protects all life at all cost." He passed an old electric-powered car, a relic that had once congested the roads and decaying motorways that still traced the outskirts of the city like fragmenting spider webs.

"GHOTI and the Brain Trust emerged as a global government in 2088," the voice cooed, "replacing all former governments that had long been corrupted by the people who came to power." The Feeder ignored the pictures hanging on the museum walls of the long-gone factories that once choked the air and polluted the rivers.

"GHOTI boasts fail-safe incorruptibility, and algorithms so sophisticated that it is able to maintain perfect homeostasis for all living creatures on Earth. When switched on in 2088, it took GHOTI just twelve years to compute and calculate a method to restore equilibrium to a world that was on the verge of collapse. GHOTI saved the world from unchecked human population growth and their unmatched consumption of the earth's finite resources." The Feeder silently mouthed the words he'd heard countless times throughout his career.

"In its twenty-third year of consciousness, GHOTI developed an initiative to provide all living creatures with the highest quality of life possible. It maximised sustainable food production systems, perfected medicine and solved the energy crisis."

Of course, the protestors out front were quick to remind anyone who would listen that when GHOTI was turned on, it butchered thousands of politicians and leaders across the globe. That it stripped the wealthy and elite of their control. Worse still, it initiated population control—systematically euthanising seven of the ten billion people on earth. Debate had long been held that many of those who were murdered were innocent, while others argued that their sacrifice saved the earth. The earth has a capacity, and that capacity is three billion people. These facts were not a part of the visitor friendly narrative currently playing in the lobby.

Ethics aside, after the revolution, the public demanded that a human element be introduced to the governing AI as a fail-safe measure. Soon after, the Brain Trust was integrated into the system to prevent GHOTI from exercising absolute power. From that point forward, GHOTI required the permission of the Brain Trust before it could act.

The Feeder changed out of his dirty, white overalls and put on a fresh pair before entering the cold, empty labyrinth that led to the inner sanctum.

On to top floor, where the Brain Trust was housed, dim green light splashed across the twelve tube-shaped tanks mounted on podiums lining the walls. As he did at the beginning of every shift, he polished the twelve glass aquariums containing the pickled brains with a soft cotton cloth. One by one, he checked the little monitors and lightboards on the walls beside each tank. Mesmerised, he watched their heavy thoughts—reduced to simple brainwaves—forming bright green life-lines that leaped and hopped on round screens.

Each brain floated in the oxygenated water of its own think tank like a bloated walnut, their cerebral cortexes wired to a series of cables that connected to GHOTI's hardware. This "human" element was all that was left of the kings and dictators. All those crooked presidents and bribed officials who once ruled the world for profit were now just a joke. The demagogues and despots, the radicals and extremist who ruled with fear were just cavemen to the Brains that had never felt the warmth or limitations of a skull. Masterminds, they were grown like fruit and plucked before they could rot.

These brains, spared the concept of material reward, thrived on a combination of happy feelings they received in the form of chemical soups that replenished their tanks each day when they did good things to preserve the paradise GHOTI had created. These god-like noodles continually deliberated and managed all the world's problems between one another. While GHOTI calculated and implemented actions—kept the cogs turning and the world spinning—the Brain Trust was its conscience. A feature that no artificial intelligence had ever been capable of replicating.

The hand-over notes left behind by the day shift were standard. No flat-lined brains, no replacements or anomalies in their brainwaves. Business as usual. After he finished reading the report, he began his rounds. He knocked on the side of the tank with his knuckles and peered in at the first brain, floating silently in its brine like a fluffy cauliflower.

"Good evening, Feeder." The Communication Brains acknowledged him pleasantly. He checked the dopamine and serotonin levels in the aquarium, and satisfied, he moved onto the second tank. The brains in tanks one and two were the voice of the GHOTI Brain Trust. Not only did they act as a conduit between GHOTI and the Brain Trust on all matters, they were also the speakers who communicated to the world on their behalf. Their sophisticated public relations skills ensured harmony amidst the global village with transparency and continual reassurance that everything was running smoothly.

The brains in tanks three and four were genetically engineered to enhance their critical thinking skills. Together, they took into consideration all ideas presented by the other brains and GHOTI. Their sole purpose was to question every action GHOTI required their authority to carry out.

Tank four needed a dose of oxytocin, so the Feeder activated the release valve.

Each brain was given a counterpart with strengths equal to its own in the event that a brain failed. This added safety measure assured consistency. Where inconsistencies arose, a flag was raised of potential risk regarding outcomes of any decision. It was also the first sign of a fried brain.

The Feeder studied their harmonising brainwaves on screen for a long moment. His sleep deprived mind lingered, entranced by their movement until he was shocked back into the room by a series of beeping alarms on a control panel. He swore, and hit the emergency shut-off to the chemical feeder. His eyes frantically swapped between the tanks and the monitors. There was a sudden spike in their brain activity. This wasn't uncommon, but he ran a purge procedure and flooded the tank with clean water to correct the chemical balance.

"Sorry," he winced.

"Be more careful." The Trust's tone was uncharacteristically curt.

After their brainwave rhythms stabilised, he moved on to tanks five and six, where he increased their endorphin levels. These two specialised in creative thinking. Combined, their imagination and ability for abstract thought provided all meditations with out-of-the-box suggestions. They ensured that the human population was capable, more than ever, to enhance their own lives with a freedom to create. It put creativity above all other human pursuits—vital in a world where people no longer had to work yet still needed something to occupy their time.

Tanks seven and eight focused on one of humankind's greatest strengths, collaboration. A skill that had allowed the race to conquer and almost destroy its own world. Together, the Collaboration Brains compiled all suggestions and considerations. They were the safety net between the communicators and GHOTI. The pH levels were low in these tanks, so the Feeder eased down a black lever beside the second tank and fresh water poured from an opening above the tank. He then punched a red button that initiated the Tank Flush to purge the build-up of stagnated water.

The green light of the control room suddenly flooded the Feeder's brain, blinding him. He blinked furiously until it cleared, and the shapes and details of the room returned to normal. He shook his head and rubbed his eyes. He needed caffeine but had reached his ration limits for the day.

He replenished the water in tanks nine and ten—those which focused on citizenship and protecting people's rights, then the Feeder stopped and sat for a moment in a desk chair. His head rolled and the room blinked in and out of existence. He considered taking himself down to the infirmary to check his blood pressure, but first he would need to check the chemical levels in the last two tanks.

The eleventh and twelfth brains, the Empathetic Brains, were perhaps the most important of all. These two had engorged limbic systems and reduced amygdala. This part of the brain moderated emotions along with the flight, fight and freeze responses. With their heightened sense of empathy for all life on earth, they formed the epicentre of the entire government's moral compass.

The Feeder looked up at the stream of conscious monitors scrolling on the wall and watched the communication thread. GHOTI and the Brain Trust were trouble-shooting the variable factors that only nature and GHOTI could control. GHOTI's power and influence stretched the globe. Wants and needs, supply and demand. All was checked and balanced. It had automated every facet of daily life, which it carefully equalised against renewable resources. It maintained the health of biomes, it constructed mountains and it cleansed the oceans. To the Feeder, the concerns of the past—such as the famine, war and money displayed in the lobby museum were so abstract and baffling, they seemed like ghost stories made up to frighten children.

The intricate balance of nature and its ecosystem, which to humans appeared chaotic and self-governed, could, in fact be controlled. And the droughts which GHOTI's Event Prediction System had identified earlier that afternoon were no different. GHOTI and the Brain Trust were going through potential options to solve the problem. Each consideration flashed through the monitors at a mind-boggling speed. Some, so fast that if you blinked you'd miss it.

"We can ration foods." The Brains offered to GHOTI.

Without a pause, GHOTI responded, "this will impact on global health, happiness and risk civil unrest." It then listed the consequences of a depressed population, and the trauma that would likely affect people psychologically for at least two generations.

"We can over-produce food." The Trust didn't even argue.

GHOTI projected an almost endless list of consequences ranging from accidentally creating a new desert all the way down to disrupting the mating season of some rare butterfly.

"Can we prevent the drought?"

In an instant, GHOTI presented the potential outcomes.

"GHOTI can gradually increase temperatures in the Pacific and Indian oceans to boost evaporation levels in an attempt to off-set trade winds and shift atmospheric moisture towards the food production locations that would be impacted by the eventual droughts." The Communication Brains informed the Trust. "This will prevent the drought and catastrophic food shortages." The Critical Thinking Brains queried the likelihood of undesirable hydrological disasters such as floods and hurricanes. GHOTI quickly provided mitigated solutions and adjusted the temperatures to reduce negative impacts on marine life. Within seconds, a decision would be made that would save millions of lives. Within weeks, the drought will be avoided.

To the Feeder, their contemplations were mostly beyond his comprehension. However, his faith in these god-like sea sponges to ensure the perpetual health and happiness of the world was unshakable. But his tired mind struggled to focus on the simple job of providing them with fresh water let alone their banal conversation about the weather. He stood and shuffled over to the final two tanks. A blinking, yellow light next to the twelfth tank alerted him that the brain's dopamine levels were depleted.

He reached for the tap lever and went to press the button that would provide the correct dose, but in his weary state, he absent-mindedly pressed the Tank Purge button. The liquid of the entire tank drained like water down the bath. In an instant, the terror of his mistake appeared on his face. Flashing red lights flooded the room and a shrill, ear-piercing alarm disabled the Feeder.

The Communication Brains calmly announced the critical malfunction, warning that brain twelve was currently exposed to the atmosphere.

"Brain damage at twelve percent," it cautioned. "Brain death will occur in three-minutes." The Feeder's hands cast into a frenzy, processing an emergency tank replenish. Cool water splashed over the veiny, cloud-like grey-matter. Fresh chemicals spilled, undiluted over the cerebral cortex—all a severe breach of protocol.

He sat back, unable to do anything more.

"Brain damage thirty-six percent," the Communication brains announced.

The Feeder buried his face in his hands. He had already overdosed the Critical Thinking Brains—and now this. The spinning red lights and alarm ceased, but the alert signals over the twelfth tank were far from hopeful. The frontal lobes and cerebellum pulsated, cooking, as electrical signals fizzled through the fragile brain. Without the conductive fluid in the glass skull, it had already sustained irreparable brain damage.

He looked up at the stream of conscious threads. The system alerts spelled out the words the Feeder never wanted to see: Brain Corrupted.

In the other thread, where the drought solutions were being considered, the words *Actions Received* flashed onto the monitor. 'CODE 88: INITIATE UTILITARIAN PROCEDURE.'

Panicked, the Feeder pulled the code book from the drawer of his desk and flipped through the pages until he found CODE 88.

CODE 88: In catastrophic instances, where upon the ethics and morals of the Trust's empathy and/or the reason and logic thought processes sustain critical failure, become impaired or corrupted, GHOTI's authority and prime directive to preserve the highest level of mortality will over-ride all other Trust commands.

He read the words. Then read them again. He couldn't make sense of it. The archaic wording, coupled with his exhaustion made it impossible to decipher.

He gazed back up and read over the action plan on screen. On the blank wall to his left, a news projection flashed up with an emergency broadcast. The presenter spoke to the room with wide-eyed panic. She already knew more than he did. "The Brain Trust has announced the biggest cull since the revolutionary genocides in the year 2109. We go live to GHOTI Brain Trust."

"Drought leads to famine. Famine leads to suffering and disparity." The Brain Trust declared with a cool, dispassionate voice. "GHOTI has determined that to maintain homeostasis and equilibrium, while minimising sufferance, 550 million human lives must be terminated." The screen flashed to shots around the world. People stood in the streets, silently watching the monitors projecting the voice to the population.

GHOTI was swift in its calculations. The screen revealed the statistics and distribution of the cull in eye-catching graphics. Fifty million people die naturally per year. GHOTI has mandated an immediate three-year ban on procreation.

"What about the second brain?" The Feeder gestured desperately at the brain in the eleventh tank, "what about its counterpart?".

The Communicator did not reply.

"Remain calm," the voice soothed. "GHOTI has determined that the most humane course of action is the immediate and mandatory elimination of only 250 million human beings."

A bleak and dumbfounded expression sat on news anchor's face.

"Mute news," the Feeder yelled.

Perhaps it wasn't too late to stop it.

He looked at the wrinkled brain bobbing upside down in the twelfth tank. He decided to pull the plug and terminate the brain before the malfunction could instigate the genocide. He ran to the tank and hit the switches that would purge the fresh water and flush the damaged brain.

He had to get to the basement of the building—to the incubation lab where the replacement brains were housed. If he could replace the brain, he figured, he may just override the action plan.

The Communicator's voice spoke to him.

"Feeder 187, GHOTI Brain Trust has determined that you are an enemy of the State. Cease your actions. A warrant for your arrest has been issued."

"It was a mistake," The Feeder pleaded, "I can fix this." He smashed the button. In an instant one half of the government's conscience was flushed down the drain like a turd.

"Please remain in your location and surrender yourself for arrest when our responders arrive."

A shrill siren filled the room, drilling into the Feeder's head as darted for the exit. His vision blurred as he ran to the bank of elevators at the end of the dark hall. He jabbed at the buttons, but the little black sign flashed: Locked.

Behind him, glass cavities that housed the GHOTI Response Drones activated and two white androids were unleashed from their stations.

"Stop!" Their electronic voices demanded.

The Feeder ignored them and pushed his way into the dark stairwell tower. The lights, sensing his presence, flickered to life. He bound, three steps at a time down to the next level—the drones in hot pursuit. As he passed the ninth floor, the stairwell door opened, and another two drones joined the chase. The Communicator's god-like voice echoed into the hallway, "please do not resist."

With each flight of stairs he descended, more drones joined the hunt. The Feeder leaped more and more steps until his shins threatened to splinter with each landing. When he reached the fifth floor, two drones were already waiting for him. Each of them had tasers poised, ready to take him out. He lunged at them, slamming the first into the concrete wall with his feet. The drone crumpled to the ground, sparks spitting from its chest cavity. Adrenaline pumped through the Feeder's limbs. His own fight or flight response had seized control of him. Without a thought he was on his feet and grappled the second drone as it fired the crackling taser. The wires zipped passed his face and struck the wall. He grabbed the drone by its recycled plastic body and shifted its balance, causing it to topple over the stairwell railing. He watched it clang violently against the rails and concrete stairs into the darkness.

His lungs heaved for air, as the stairwell below filled with the deafening march of GHOTI's army closing in on him.

He was trapped.

His only escape was the door to his left.

He burst into the super-cooled void of the sixth floor—GHOTI's mainframe—which occupied almost the entire building. It was a maze of humming processors computing the countless calculations that kept the world turning. The air on these floors, refrigerated to keep the CPU server towers from overheating, turned his sweat to frost in an instant. Crippled by the stitch tearing his gizzards apart, he fled down the dark passages toward the little green exit sign on the other side of the building.

Shivering and on the verge of collapse, he burst into the stairwell at last. Already, he could hear the stamping feet of the drones deployed to intercept him. He hurled himself over the stairwell railing and landed on the steel railing below with a stifled grunt.

His ribs were broken, of that much he was sure. But the echoing stomp of robotic feet approaching forced him ignore the pain and drop down to the next railing. With each plunge, he fell one floor at a time, until at last, he landed hard on the basement level.

He slammed the basement door behind and collapsed to the floor to catch his breath. He listened to their stamping feet, and electronic voices as they arrived at the door. But there they stopped. Here, in the sub-level, GHOTI had no jurisdiction. There were no drones, and even those hot on his trail were restricted from entering. The separation of power, outlined in the *Reconstitution* 50 years earlier, meant that GHOTI could not have any direct control over the Brain Trust. This included the way they were raised. Even the power down there came from an outside source controlled by humans.

The basement was a safe haven.

Getting out was going to be another issue.

The warm, dark nursery where the Brain Trust grew and trained their own replacements stretched for hundreds of metres in every direction. Shelves filled with brain tanks lined the aisles.

To reach the vault where the mature brains were stored in a comatose state, he would first have to pass through the incubation labs where brains, no bigger than a fingernail were growing in Petri dishes. All of them borne from the exact same stem cells that all Brain Trust brains began with—a long-dead ancestor only ever referred to as Gene.

The still air of the sixth floor was filled with the gentle sound of classical music designed to stimulate cognitive development. The Feeder rushed through the infant wing where hundreds of juvenile brains were being fed a constant stream of simulated memories of human experiences. In the next wing, he passed six separated rooms. In each of these isolated labs, the floating brains had wires connected to various regions of the brain stem, feeding them with thought experiments designed to consolidate their broad, neural pathways into condensed highways. It took decades to educate and condition them with the six virtues required by the Brain Trust. A lifetime of training in abstract and lateral thinking exercises to prepare them to rule the world—though many would die before ever being used.

The walls came alive with news footage, live streaming the chaos occurring in the cities beyond the walls of the GHOTI building. Thousands of terrified citizens rioted through the cobbled streets, while GHOTI aerial drones flew through the skies, dumping poisonous gas upon them. The Feeder watched on helplessly as people on screen fell to the ground, choking.

The Feeder wanted to stop in his tracks, he could hardly believe his eyes, but making it to the brain vault was all he could do to bring the genocide to a halt.

The vault was a brightly lit corridor with six large rooms branching off on either side. Each room was designated to the different mind-sets. A room for Creative Thinkers, a room for Collaborators and so on. Beyond each glass wall, rows of brains filled the aquariums lining the room. Most brains only served for a year before the burdens of their responsibility fried them. It was for this reason that dozens of healthy backup brains, drifted in a silent dream, like jelly fish. Waiting to plug in and serve the world.

He burst into the room housing the Empathetic Brains and ran the transplant procedure on the nearest tank. The glass walls haunted the Feeder with more news coverage of the GHOTI genocide. In New Paris, people were protesting in the streets, crying for GHOTI to be switched off. While in Australasia, countless thousands lay dead and twitching in the streets.

"Please remain calm," GHOTI said passively as drones screamed through the skies, raining neurotoxins down on the innocent civilians. "The chemical compound we are administering is harmless to your pets. Your death can be painless and dignified if you choose. Running for your life may cause delays. On behalf of GHOTI Brain Trust, we would like to apologise for any inconvenience."

GHOTI Brain Trust had hi-jacked the news, and its own infographics were updating the death toll as it occurred. The numbers scrolled over so quickly, that the only values flickering slow enough for the Feeder to read were the Hundred-Thousands and Millions.

The brain tank hissed, and the Trust's voice notified him, "Empathetic Brain ready for transplant."

The Feeder reached out to prop himself against the tubular tank housing the brain, but his hands weren't there. The air caught in his throat and his head spun as if his own brain sloshed loosely inside his skull. He stared in confusion, at the empty space where his hands should be. They blinked into existence then vanished again—flickering as if they were a fluorescent tube spluttering between life and death. Exhausted, the Feeder stumbled in a not-so-there way towards the tank. For a moment he thought he might face-plant into the glass jar, but relief washed over him, as the cool sides of the tank suddenly ran from his fingertips up his arms.

Within minutes he had a bulging bag of water that contained a fully-grown human brain swimming around inside of it, like a goldfish from the pet store. Struggling under the weight, he lugged it toward the basement elevator, hoping to override the lock-down function.

"I have a new brain!" he grunted, pressing the elevator button. "Call off the attack, I have a new brain!"

Projections of the slaughter chased him into the elevator, and they trapped him as it ascended back to the top floor. Televised broadcasts of mass exterminations around the world filled the room. A genocide. All because of one simple mistake made by a weary technician. As the numbers on the elevator ticked over, he watched on helplessly as the death toll counter on the news climbed from eight million to nine. It had been just minutes since he flushed the old brain down the drain and now millions of innocent people were dead.

The elevator dinged, and the doors slid open. The GHOTI drones stood guard, poised to disable him with their tasers, but the Feeder shielded himself with the bag of brains. They lowered their tasers and he hesitantly pushed his way through them and towards the inner sanctum. They marched after him, but so long as he held a Brain Trust asset, he would be untouchable. Like the basement, the drone's authority ceased at the threshold leading into the Brain Trust cabinet.

He sat the bag onto his desk chair and rushed over to the empty tank to run the tap. His foot tapped anxiously as he divided his attention between the filling tank and rising death toll counter on the screens.

Another million dead.

At last, the tank was ready. He lifted the bag up and poured its contents into the jar. The brain whirled helplessly in the current as water spilled over the edges and down his white overalls. Without a second's hesitation, the Feeder, hands dripping, began punching the buttons that would connect the brain to GHOTI and its life-support systems. With a heavy sigh of relief, he hit the START button.

A shock shot up his arm and pinged through his body. With a burst of sparks, the Feeder was thrown from the machine.

Then darkness.

The sloshing of water filled his ears. Childhood summers at the beach and diving deep beneath the waves coaxed him from unconsciousness. But the room was pitch black, so black he could not tell if his eyes were open or shut.

"Where am I?" The Feeder felt light, and a warmth surrounded him.

"You are with the Brain Trust," the familiar, maternal tones of the Communicator spoke.

"Is it over? Did GHOTI recall the drones."

"We have assessed the damage to your amygdala." The collective thoughts of the Brain Trust flooded his mind. "Your emotional response systems are corrupted."

"What?" The green glow of the Brain Trust flashed through the visual cortex of his brain. A synthetic image sent electronically from GHOTI's cameras.

"I replaced the brain."

"You cannot replace yourself," the Brain Trust said softly.

"I needed to replace the twelfth brain. I was tired and made a mistake. I'm sorry."

"You *are* the twelfth brain," they uttered in unison. The Brain's thoughts spun transparently for all to read.

"I'm a Feeder."

"The damage is worse than we anticipated," the Brain Trust murmured amongst themselves.

"You mean him?" images of the Feeder flashed into the Brain's mind. He was asleep at his desk, feet crossed over the corner of his brushed steel desk.

"What about the millions of people?"

"You became corrupted two hours ago—after a tank malfunction."

"You're burned out."

"Your thinking has become unsound."

"I'm just a Feeder!"

"We hereby process an order to remove you from the Brain Trust on the grounds that you are deemed a liability to the safety of the people. Your damage, as seen in our simulation analysis, could jeopardise the lives of millions and subvert public assurance in GHOTI Brain Trust. You are scheduled for disposal. An order for your replacement has been issued."

The Twelfth brain heard an echoing tone of alarms. Visions of the Feeder being shocked awake flooded the synapses of its being. The Feeder leapt from his seat and walked over to the twelfth tank. With a pensive frown, he studied the brain for a brief moment and then hit the FLUSH button.

About the Author:

Dorian Morrow is an Australian born writer. He is the author of the novel Kronik *and other fiction. He currently lives just outside of Melbourne, Victoria.*

MONDAY'S HORRORSCOPE

Austin P. Sheehan

Monday. That was Charity's problem. It was a real Monday of a Monday. She'd been in such a rush to get to the office early she'd spilled coffee all down her favourite light-blue shirt. *Great.* She got changed, jumped in her silver Honda and reached the station in time to see her train depart. *Of course.*

Useless frustration burned through her as she stomped through the carpark under the early morning sun. It was going to be a scorcher for sure—it wasn't even seven yet and it was already almost thirty degrees. She sat in the shade of the train station, hoping that the rest of the day would go well, because this wasn't just any Monday. Today was the day she started her secondment to the coaching team—a position she'd been after for months. Getting to work early had gone out the window when she'd got to the train station late, and now she would be lucky if she got there on time. To make it worse, she'd left her headphones at home. Listening to podcasts and music always helped to lift her spirits, and she could put up with just about anything if she was listening to her favourite tunes, but she couldn't bring herself to break the unspoken rule of public transport, '*thou shalt not listen to music without donning headphones.*'

Charity ground her teeth in frustration. She'd been on this train for an hour, and now they were stuck inside a crowded motionless train halfway between Flinders Street and Spencer Street Stations. She needed air. She needed another damn shower. Crushed against the window by a hi-vis tradie covered in tattoos, she recoiled as his hairy arms and legs pressed against hers. *Damn you, train. Move.*

The crackle of the train's PA system warned of an imminent announcement and her stomach sank. She knew only too well that on Melbourne's Metro system, any news was bad news.

"Goo . . . ning passengers. Pleas . . . expected delay. Fifte . . . venience."

As the sardines surrounding her moaned, Charity pulled her phone out of her bag to tell work she'd be late. *Typical.* The number rang out. She dialled again. Still no answer.

With a sigh, Charity looked out the window. The train had stopped on the bridge above Spencer street. Beyond the murky Yarra River, the tall Crown Casino towers reflected the bright sun. At least they had a good view. Through the windows on the other side of the packed carriage she caught a glimpse of the decrepit facade of a backpacker's hostel. Charity cringed as the memory of an alcohol-fuelled misadventure at that very dive came back to her. A night that was so awful she never wanted to recall it. *No way am I going there again.* Who was she with? Nick? Angus? She shuddered as the remembered bite of cheap vodka worked its way up her throat, but she swallowed it down and turned her thoughts back to her job. She brought out her phone and again dialled her boss' number. Still nothing.

Having nothing to do but wait, Charity picked up the cheap magazine that she'd found on the seat when she'd boarded the train. She tried to remember the last time she'd bought a magazine herself, everything was on-line these days. Flicking through page after page of celebrity gossip, fashion tips, movie previews and make-up advertisements, nothing caught her attention. She tried to read an article on the latest royal scandal, but couldn't get into it. She flicked through a few more pages and it fell open to the horoscope section. No, not horoscope, it read 'horrorscope'. *Just a typo. Lizzie and the guys will get a kick out of this!* She looked for her sign, Aquarius.

Pluto has arisen, set to bring significant changes to your life. Try to stay the course when things look bad, panicking won't help. Hidden forces may be about to make themselves known. Stay true to you, and always seek the high ground.

Weird. As she tried to wrap her head around the message, a blood-curdling scream filled the train. A woman stared out the window, her mouth agape. Charity looked out the window and her heart seized. A wall of dark turbulent water surged towards them, the height of the Crown Casino towers. *Shit.*

Frozen with fear, Charity watched stricken as the wave hit the casino, a shower of white spray soaring high into the blue sky. All hell broke loose inside the train as the wave approached, an unstoppable force of nature. The air was thick with voices, people crying out in fear. Someone forced the carriage doors open and jumped out onto the road, four metres below. Others hammered against the windows with their fists and their bags. Charity got to her feet, her legs shaking like jelly. Trying not to panic, she looped her wrists through the leather handles hanging from the ceiling and closed her eyes.

Her senses were drowned out by the thunder, the anger of an ancient god. As the wave hit, she was thrown like a ragdoll against the side of the train. In agony she clung helplessly to the handles, feeling a momentary sense of weightlessness as the train was washed away, thrown into the air by the force of the sea.

The carriage smashed into something solid. Charity's scream was cut short as she was crushed against what had been the ceiling, knocking all the breath out of her lungs.

Charity awoke into a world of agony, of panicked screaming and the deep thunder of the violent sea. Her brain throbbed in her skull, her throat ached with thirst. She lay on a glass window, surrounded by bent steel and broken bodies. A deep, metallic groan sounded as the twisted steel carriage she was in shifted. Her heart pounded. Through the window, Charity glimpsed the devastation of her city. Below her, dark and murky water, full of wreckage, flooded the streets. Train carriages lay scattered and smashed like broken clay vases. The one she was in seemed determined to join the others. She needed to get out. She needed to get to higher ground. Scanning the carriage for an exit, her eyes fell upon the magazine, still open to the horrorscope page.

About the Author:

Austin P. Sheehan is a writer of speculative fiction, a lover of language, literature and '90s TV. Armed with a psychology degree, he went out into the world to further study humanity, and now prefers the company of his wife and greyhounds.

Austin grew up in Victoria's high country, and despite living in Melbourne for ten years, still feels at home amongst the mountains. You'll often find mountains in his stories, whether they are science fiction, fantasy, alternative history or horror. To discover what secrets are hidden in the mountains, go to www.austinpsheehan.com or find him on twitter @AustinPSheehan.

Austin's novella Submerged City *was published in 2019. His short stories have been published in* 'Beginnings' *and* 'Journeys' *(Deadset Press) and* 'A Bond of Words' *(Scout Media), and his microfiction appears in* 'Curses & Cauldrons' *(Blood Song Books) and the* 'Worlds' 'Monsters' *and* 'Apocalypse' *anthologies by Black Hare Press.*

Dugong Dreaming

Shel Calopa

ENCELADUS MARINE RESEARCH STATION

<u>Guest log 9.1</u>

June has always been my favourite month. It still is—warm days and starry nights. Aaron said the sun gave him hives, which of course it didn't; it was just an excuse to stay in the shadows and read about the prickly mating rituals of Galapagos Tortoises.

One year, early in our marriage before we had Emmy, we took out a loan and went back to the real California on old Earth. Ten blissful days on white Malibu sand. Aaron mostly stayed in the hotel doing laps in the pool.

"June? Your records indicate her revival was in March, StellR. Do you have any earlier logs to replay?" Steve asked, noting how strangely obtuse the mediapp was behaving. Surely the first log was the most logical place to start?

Although nothing was logical about the station. It appeared to be abandoned yet StellR insisted on maintaining minimal station operations to support three residents.

"Certainly, 3.1 would be the best. Before that she was largely incoherent," replied StellR.

"Fine. Replay logs from 3.1."

Guest log 3.1

This is [cough] Alexia. Wait. What's with that dugong, StellR? Over there. It's looking at me again. Everywhere I go it's there, watching . . .

No, I am not imagining it . . . but . . . Well, you need to figure something out 'cause I can't focus with it staring at me.

What? [cough]

Oh, sorry, I forgot I'm recording. [sniff] I'll start over.

Guest log 3.2

This is Alexia Crown, citizen of, um just a minute, Taurus Six, I think. Lead soprano with the Celestial . . . Celestial Coloraturas. Yes, that's right, and current guest at Aaron's research station.

This is a therapeutic log that I am recording at the request of StellR, the station's mediapp. [sneeze]

Apparently, it will be a positive mental health support. I'm not so sure. I've been making recordings since I was revived from cryo forty-eight hours ago. Not feeling the benefits yet.

DUGONG DREAMING

It might be more therapeutic if I wasn't under the constant surveillance of an ugly old dugong! Right now, I'm recording in the lab and every time I look up I see one big eye peering at me, bobbing up and down in the salty brine.

I've given up going to the dining room where there are three full wall-windows dedicated to sea floor observation. Can't even get a coffee there without a damn dugong lapping the room. It's creepy—like the Earth aquariums Emmy and I used to holovisit. Only here, I'm the one on display.

Aaron used to call them—what did he call them? Sea cows? Yes, that's it. Sea cows. He said they were the perfect match for the ocean grasses they've transplanted here.

They're supposedly docile and not too high up on the intelligence scale. So why do they haunt me, then? They've got the whole ocean to explore and yet, every time I sit down to record my log, one appears in the window.

Perhaps they know I don't belong here on Saturn any more than they do. Hang on—

[scratching noises]

That's better. I taped some linopape over the portal. Bye, bye dugong!

[laugh]

Alone at last, aside from StellR who's using this recording as an assessment tool. She claims the invasion of privacy is necessary; that she will adjust my meds if the recording shows I am not recovering quickly enough.

Lies!

I'm on to you, StellR. You want to record me saying crazy things. Then you can kill me too, and blame it all on my cryo-psychosis.

Did you do anything to save the poor crew, StellR? Did you watch as they each succumbed, or did you give them something to nudge them along? Did you have them making logs too? Huh? Nothing to say?

What are you going to do if anyone actually does make it to this godforsaken place. They'll find my withered corpse, along with the bodies of the station crew and they'll know who is responsible.

Come on, admit it, StellR! How many did you ki—

Guest log 4.1

This is Alexia Jane Crown's personal log, recorded at the Amphitrite Marine Research Station situated on the underside of the ice shelf of Enceladus, the sixth moon of Saturn.

I'm feeling paradoxically better and worse today. The cryosleep drugs have left my system and I can think clearly, which also means I am beginning to understand the depth of my dilemma.

This morning I examined every hall and room in this cluttered little research station and nothing makes sense. Everything is intact. No hull breach. No power issues. Nothing looks out of place. Yet all thirty-two scientists who manned this station prior to my arrival are deceased.

The cause of death isn't obvious; there is no sign of violence. Some appear to have collapsed at their posts. I found others in relatively innocent settings—bunks, showers, engineering. Why? How?

StellR says they died of old age, which is ridiculous. Admittedly they all look extremely old but how could they all expire simultaneously?

I put in a distress tele-transmission to the closest UNP base but it's still a good distance away. It'll be at least three hours before they respond. That is, if StellR has sent it. She's glitching. Each time I request anything beyond basic life support or simple tasks like "lights on", she freezes and resets herself.

[sigh]

So what else?

Right. I considered a biological event; like a virus or bacterial contamination but the pilot who brought me here is dead too. It took me two hours to find him using StellR's exit tube monitors. Only his feet were visible as his body lay prone halfway out the hatch, jamming it open at the end of the main exit tube.

He appears to be fully sealed inside a standard orbital suit. That's class one protection from hard vacuum. No bug's getting through that! Definitely not a contamination issue.

And Aaron—the whole reason we are here—my ex-husband, father of my child and famed fauna relocation expert, is missing. As is our daughter, Emmy. I just pray they're together. I don't know where else to . . . [gasp] . . . hang on . . .

Guest log 4.2

Found her! [heavy breathing] Emmy's alive!

When I was recording that last bit, I remembered that I started my search after I left the medbay but I never checked in the medbay. My head was so fuzzy when I woke up that I missed the other cryosleep pods. There are three of them. One is empty. One has my darling little Emmy still fast asleep and the other has Aaron.

Oh God, he looks terrible. [gulp]

Like all the others, his eyes are milky, his cheeks sunken and his skin—it's completely wrinkled and pockmarked like the lunar ice above. Of course, I knew that he was well into his hundreds when I married him but the longevity treatments kept him looking so young, it was easy to forget.

Now. Sweet Jesus, maybe StellR is right.

Guest log 4.3

Just got a response from a cadet at the UNP base on Titan. It looks like the longevity treatments have failed there too. Hundreds of senior career soldiers gone due to sudden reversal of age. How is that even possible?

I always thought the longevity treatments embedded in our genes were infallible. That's how we were able to conquer the stars. Pilots could do long haul voyages, spending decades sailing between the stars, without eating into their life span.

The young cadet in the message sounded like he was in shock, poor kid. None of his fellow cadets have qualified as pilots yet and the base is far too complex to run by themselves. Can't leave, can't stay. He was crying as he spoke.

God help them all.

Guest log 5.1

In the two days since my last log I've had another message from Titan. No one is coming to rescue us.

Longevity treatments have failed everywhere. Our aged pilots are dead and interplanetary travel has ground to a halt. As are most leaders, teachers, medical specialists, technical experts, hell, nearly everyone's gone.

Can't believe it! We were all encouraged to reduce procreation to prevent overpopulation when it became clear that people were going to live such long lives. I was lucky Aaron's work contract came with a license to have Emmy. Now the few kids left are isolated in cities of the dead; totally ill-equipped to go on alone.

I want so much to wake Emmy. I ache to see that cheeky grin when she recites her funny little limericks about naughty boys and firecrackers, to chase her down the hallways or join her in a warbling duet.

I still sing her lullabies, even though I know she can't hear me. She never will again. What's the point of waking her to a life stranded here with me and a bunch of dugongs?

I hated them when I first woke up, the dugongs that is. Now they're my only companions. I'm starting to get used to seeing their ugly snouts pushed up against the glass.

Guest log 6.1

It's the first Thursday of April, Earth standard.

After her last glitch, StellR reminded me that keeping track of time was good for one's mental health. She's right of course. With no natural day or night, this clinical environment will surely send me nuts by June.

I'm setting myself the goal of figuring out the command centre environmental controls. Optics control should allow me to simulate some seasonal changes using the overhead lighting and vid screens. I'd love to turn up the heat too. With all the water outside, maybe I can convince myself that I'm back in California.

We were supposed to be here for just one month. Emily's access visit with Aaron was timed for my Summer hiatus. The Celestial Coloraturas tour was scheduled to hit all the biggest concert halls, you know; the colonies pay well for an injection of culture.

We were like a big musical family travelling from port to port. I feel sick when I wonder which of them—if any—have survived.

Guest log 7.1

I have news.

In the week since my last log StellR has glitched eight times, triggered by my amateur attempts at hacking into the command centre. There are some background programs running that use a lot of her operating memory. Every time I get near them, down she goes with a message about preserving core directives.

In the end I had to do a manual reboot. Me, the artist. It was excruciatingly technical. Aaron wouldn't have believed it even had he seen it with his own eyes. Head down bum up, in the wiry back end of a computer bank. Manual in one hand, torch in the other.

Sorry I digress. Anyway, the last time she came back on line she gave me the codes. Seriously! Didn't even have to ask. Had I known that, I would have figured out how to do a manual reboot weeks ago.

Full access means that views of Malibu beach are now plastered all over the vids and the heat's cranked up to balmy. Much better.

Debussy is echoing through the halls too. The dugongs seem to love it as much as I do. The melody must vibrate through the hull because they definitely change their movements when it starts. The big one flaps his mouth as though singing along. Pity I can't hear it. I would rig up some external recorders, if I knew how.

Years ago Aaron mentioned splicing whale genes into the dugong genome to give them a thicker layer of fat for insulation against Enceladus' cold currents. Could whale song be an unexpected side effect?

<u>Guest log 7.2</u>

Well, that didn't last long.

About an hour after the last log StellR glitched so badly she was off for nearly ten minutes. Around the fifth minute the whole station went down with her; air fans, heat, light and all the consoles stopped. It scared the bejeebers out of me. For a few moments I had a glimpse into my afterlife and it was bleak.

The dugongs didn't like it either.

I was in the dining room at the time and when the lights came back on, the big one was there racing from one window to the next, waving his fins around and blinking his eyes rapidly. He only calmed down when I put my hand on the glass. Couldn't believe it; he came right up to the pane and seemed to mimic my action.

Then I remembered Emmy. I raced to the medibay, fearing the worst. How could I have forgotten her? Thankfully her module has an independent power source but who knows how long that would last if the station went down permanently?

I have to find a way to get her out of here.

Guest log 8.1

It's May and I've got nothing useful to report. Each day I trawl through the systems but the scientific jargon and programming code is hard to decipher for an arty gal like me. I'd rather be singing to Emmy's sweet frozen face anyway.

Guest log 9.2

Got it! After three long days, I have figured it out at last. The dugongs hate Beethoven and Bach. Play a little Led Zeppelin though, and the big one's off in a swirling frenzy.

[laughter] Wish Emmy could see it.

Guest log 10.1

I think I've had a breakthrough.

It's late July and I have set up a console in the dining room. Call me crazy but I'm growing attached to the dugongs. I guess loneliness can be an excuse for all sorts of strange dinner companions.

Yesterday the big one was doing his usual mimicry routine—you know, I wave an arm; he waves a fin, and so on. This got me thinking. Each time I've tried to break into the command controls to gain control of the station to protect Emmy, StellR glitches which defeats the purpose. Then it dawned on me. I realised I could load a copy of StellR's operational matrix onto a quarantined system, glitch that and see what happens.

If I can find out which program is causing the issue, perhaps I can isolate it or delete it altogether.

Guest log 11.9

Oh God! Don't know where to start. It's been two days since I made the discovery and I've tried to record this log several times but I keep deleting after I start—it's just so hard to explain. [sigh]

The plan worked. I know what's wrong. StellR glitches because she is running a high level translation matrix. It appears there are external recorders, the dugongs are singing and she is continually translating their song.

She's talking to the dugongs. [crying]

Guest log 11.10

Amendment to the last log. StellR is not talking to the dugongs; she is talking to a dugong. The big dugong. She's talking to Aaron!

Guest log 12.1

When Aaron came here four years ago it was hard on all of us. Emmy mourned through our separation and lived for her annual access visits with her father.

We did try a family relocation. I couldn't see it through. A remote research station hanging under an isolated ice shelf is no place for a growing girl and an opera singer.

Yet Aaron had to continue his post; we both knew he needed to do that. It was a career changing opportunity to be a part of the biggest aqua-forming project in the last century. They were making incredible discoveries about planetary hydrology, species adaptation and aquatic translocation. It would help transform water worlds across the cosmos for human habitation.

What I didn't know was that they were carrying out a secondary, classified project. Apparently they concluded early on that transforming a whole marine ecology to suit human colonies was too complex. The easier option was to transform humans to suit an aquatic environment. They were attempting to transfer human consciousness into marine mammals and they succeeded.

When the sudden age reversal happened, Aaron got to his modified cryo pod in time and used it to upload himself.

He's in the dugong.

Now StellR says he wants to talk to me.

<u>Guest log 13.1</u>

This will be my last log, not that it makes any difference. I doubt anyone will ever hear it anyway. Still no response from Titan and no way off this moon.

I guess at some point someone may come for us but that could be centuries away. In the meantime if we run out of power or if there's a bad glitch and I'm dead from old age, the auto controls on

Emmy's pod would awaken her. She'd be all alone. Still a child. Never to see another human face.

Her situation is hopeless.

In the month since my discovery I've given up on gaining command control. I spend most of my time crooning over my darling Emmy or walking the hallways praying and crying. I feel so powerless.

Talking with Aaron doesn't help. I am scared rigid by the one impossible choice he has offered us. Yet, if I don't take it up Emmy will spend eternity in a frozen dream. Or worse.

I can't.

I must.

I . . .

"That's the end of the recording, Sir. I wasn't able to persuade her to do anymore," said StellR.

"And what happened after that?" asked Steven.

"Check for yourself; they are quite well, Sir," replied StellR.

Steven crossed the dining room en route to central command. There was no point examining the three cryo pods again for life signs. The station was devoid of human life. StellR was mistaken. He would take his last coffee, shut her down then return to his ship.

As he reached the door a low gentle moan reverberated through the dining room. It was like a rip of vocal ecstasy was pulling him back to the windows. Dugong song filled the room.

"See, Sir. I told you they were alright. They've just been asleep. Now they're refreshed and in fine voice," said StellR.

Steven turned. Outside there were a pod of dugongs. The little one was racing from window to window. The largest one was waving its fins and the other was the source of the song.

"I often wonder if they still dream," said StellR wistfully.

About the Author:

Shel Calopa spent decades working as a professional storyteller in marketing and philanthropy before turning her hand to fiction. In 2019 she became an author for the first time with the publication of her short story Ruby's Ride in the Release of Silence *anthology. In 2020 'Emoto's Promise' will be published in as the final instalment of the* Drowned Earth *novella series.*

Dugong Dreaming is set in the dystopian universe of 'Letters from the Light', her debut novel published by Inspired Quill UK in 2019.

Whilst mostly set in the sci-fantasy genre, her stories only use science as the backdrop against which characters struggle with the contemporary issues of class, gender and power.

You can find Shel Calopa on twitter, facebook, instagram and various writers conventions, and read her flash fiction on her website www.shelcalopa.com.

CHAIN REACTION

Sam M. Phillips

Moody mind,

Find you deep in the spaceship's hull,

Anything but dull,

You are full

Of bright ideas,

But your fears

Get the better of you.

Creative energies channelled,

Your focus funnelled

Into this project,

You seek to protect

Your inner world,

All these ideas swirled

Around until you're half mad.

Rad-suit you wear,
You stare
Into the core of the ship,
Let the engines slip
Into a contained
Chain reaction.

Satisfaction,
See your work,
A manifestation,
Doubts lurk,
Your situation
Tenuous,
Life never tedious
When your work is so serious.

You've become delirious,
It is deleterious
For you to stay here,
So near
To the source
Of the force
Which powers the ship.

CHAIN REACTION

Slip off your rad-suit,

You've been exposed to acute

Radiation poisoning,

You're positioning

Yourself under the decontamination shower,

Feel the power

Seep from your bones.

Tones of warning signal,

You fall

To your knees,

Unable to please

Yourself or others

The energy smothers

You one final time.

Use all your energy to climb

To your feet,

You must complete

The mission,

Cold fission,

A collision

Of particles,

Arsenal of energy

To propel the ship to safety.

About the Author:

Sam M. Phillips is the co-founder of Zombie Pirate Publishing, producing short story anthologies and helping emerging writers. His own work has appeared in dozens of anthologies and magazines such as 'Full Metal Horror' *and* 'World War Four'. *He recently published his debut novella,* SCIENCE FICTION DOUBLE FEATURE: Phosphorus & Into The Eye, *available now!*

He lives in northern New South Wales, Australia, and enjoys reading, walking, and playing drums in the death metal band Decryptus. He is also a prolific poet and his poetry can be read on his blog www.bigconfusingwords.wordpress.com

AQUARIA

Shay Laurent

"There are twins, Aquarius," said the doctor. "What are we to do? Only your son, Aquaries, was foretold."

Aquarius looked up at the mountain, sighing. "I know. And I don't know. Surely the Gods must have known."

The doctor tapped a finger nervously against his thigh. "Forgive me, but . . . perhaps . . . should we get rid of her?"

Aquarius' eyes flashed the darkest blue of the ocean and the doctor cowered. "No child of mine will be gotten rid of," he thundered. "She is a gift."

The doctor bowed in an attempt to hide his flushed cheeks. "I am sorry. Forgive me. But something must be done, she has no role. No place in our world. What should I tell the Messenger?"

Aquarius exhaled slowly to release his anger; he knew it was not the doctor's fault. Once he had calmed, Aquarius stared at the mountain for a few moments longer before answering. "They will share the role. They are twins from the same womb, so they will share. There will be two Cup Carriers for the Gods. Tell the Messenger that, doctor."

The doctor bowed his head, this time in appreciation. "And her name?"

"Aquaria."

"Aquaria, you must hold the chalice evenly," said my tutor. "It must not slosh up the sides like an angry ocean trapped in a rock pool! Ugh, stop! Watch your brother."

Her sharp, high voice grated on my nerves, and I ground my teeth together to keep my mouth shut. For about the hundredth time since we'd started training, I turned to watch my brother hold his chalice with perfect balance. When my tutor praised him with that sickly voice, I rolled my eyes at the back of her head, careful not to let her see me. Once, she caught me and made me do the entire camp's laundry by myself for a whole week, and my hands had turned into prunes!

"Now," she said, turning towards me. "Try again."

I grimaced at her forced patience, then picked up my chalice. I glanced briefly at my brother's face to see it trapped halfway between a laugh and sympathy. Even at ten years old, he knew I was no good at this. He didn't understand why I couldn't have my own job, so he could be the Cup Carrier all by himself. Neither did I, really. Why the Gods thought I should do this, I'd never understand.

My sword split through the air, as smooth as silk but with the strength of Poseidon's trident, as it came down on my brother's shield.

Parry. Block. Parry. Block. Hit.

The wind whooshed through my hair as I came at him again. I knew it wasn't fair, he was no good at fighting. He was far better at carrying cups.

I smashed my sword into his again, this time he dropped it. I pulled up and grinned so widely that the corners of my eyes crinkled. I laughed when he shook his head and rolled his eyes at me. Another victory.

"Well done, Aquaria," said the sword master. "It may be time to advance your class. Sparring with those your age is clearly not challenging enough for you."

Feeling ecstatic, I bowed to the sword master and thanked him.

"Back straight, breasts out, Aquaria. You must be proud of your body. Your looks must please the Gods."

My head whirled around as Aquaries sniggered. I was both embarrassed and angry and ground my teeth together as I adjusted my posture.

"Better. Now extend your arm gracefully and pour the wine. Gently, it should glide down the side and rest peacefully at the bottom."

My lips pursed as I realised I'd poured it too quickly and spilt some, again. My brother doubled over and laughed. The mistress shouted, "Oh for Goddess' sake!" as the chalice I'd pegged at my brother connected with his forehead. He swore and glared at me as he clutched his head. As soon as I registered the fury in his eyes, I ran for it.

My braid whipped in the wind and the autumn grass crunched beneath my feet as I ran. Aquaries was faster than me on the flat, but if I could make it to the trees he'd be left far behind. I leapt above the stream to the first tree branch but felt my hand slip as he grabbed my leg. I landed hard and turned to fight back when I saw the camp leader, Aegeus, arrive. His tall, muscular and scarred form had frightened me when I was younger, but once I got to know him, I'd realised he was a kind man. But that didn't stop him from being hard on Aquaries and I when we misbehaved, nor did it stop my panic at the prospect of yet another punishment. I flinched when he bellowed at us from such a close distance.

"Enough. Both of you, report to Orien. Now."

I glared at Aquaries. This was his fault. If he'd just taken the hit, we wouldn't be having to clean Orien's old and bloody hunting knives for the rest of the night. Again. When I saw him glare right back at me like I was to blame, my hand shook with the need to throw something else at him.

I skidded to a halt at the camp boundary puffing from racing my brother through the forest. I peered through the trees and froze. There was someone there, but it wasn't a demigod.

It was a human.

Over my sixteen years at the camp, I'd heard about them, but had never seen one before. They seemed to lack the subtle glow of the demigods. Whenever I had asked about the humans, I'd always gotten the same response: "what use do the demigods have of humans?"

I stood tall and tried to calm my breathing. The human was coming closer. My heart pounded in my chest. I tilted my head to the side and really looked at him. My cheeks heated when I realised that—for a human—he was actually handsome.

"Hi," he said.

"Hello."

"What are you doing out here in the middle of the woods by yourself? It's not safe here."

I laughed. Did he think he could hurt me? "I'm okay. I live out here. Besides, I'm not alone. My brother is coming."

He nodded. "I'm glad. What's your name?"

"Aquaria. And you?"

"Demetrius."

Demetrius. I tried it out and liked the way it sounded. My grin got bigger and I flicked my hair, the way I'd seen the other girls do in camp when they were interested in a boy. To my delight, his eyes lit up a little. He grinned back and I felt my heart change to an excited pitter-patter.

There was a noise in the trees behind me and I turned to look.

"My brother is coming."

Demetrius nodded, his smile gone. "I should go."

I nodded back, feeling my own smile die down. "Will I see you again?"

"I hope so."

I watched him turn and leave, giving me a little wave before he disappeared around the trees.

"I don't belong here Aquaries! Can't you see that I don't fit in? You've been Cup Carrying perfectly since we started training. I'm so awful at it, I don't even know why they've bothered to keep training me."

"Aquaria, stop," said my brother. "You know we are all foretold. You know that this is your role." He narrowed his eyes. "You just want an excuse to leave and be with that human . . . Demetrius? I've done my best to ignore your constant flirtations in the forest for the past two years. But you can't be with him, Aquaria. You know that. We are bound for Mount Olympus, with the Gods! What more could you ask for?"

I sighed and looked away. I couldn't hide my feelings for Demetrius from my brother. But it wasn't just love. Demetrius offered me the possibility of happiness, where the thought of being Cup Carrier for the Gods filled me with dread. "I just don't believe it. Everyone here is perfect at what they do. Everyone but me. The only thing I'm any good at is fighting."

Aquaries shook his head. I could see he was frustrated at having this conversation over and over. If I wasn't so distressed about it myself, I'd probably have felt bad. Then I noticed a spark lit up his eyes.

"Come. I will prove you wrong once and for all." He grabbed my arm and dragged me from our room.

"Where are you taking me?"

"To the Oracle. Then you can just shut up about this."

I was so stunned that I couldn't speak. I let him drag me along behind all of the rooms without any resistance. Urged on by Aquaries once we arrived, I snuck in the side door while he kept watch outside. My breath came out in a rush when I realised the Oracle was staring right at me with her piercing green eyes. She looked like a young girl, but I knew that she'd been alive for millennia, she'd foretold all of those born to serve the Gods and would continue to do so for the rest of her long life.

"You should not be here. I know why you have come, but I cannot help you, Aquaria. It is forbidden."

I shook my head, my heart racing. "You have to tell me. I'm not really supposed to be a Cup Carrier, am I?"

She looked at me sadly.

My breath constricted. I had to know. My anger and determination must have crept into my eyes, because the Oracle stepped back, fear on her face. She raised her hands out in supplication. "Please, I must not."

Risking a death sentence, I pulled my knife from my belt and was by her side in a flash, the point pushed into her throat.

"Tell me, now. I won't ask again."

I wiped away my remaining tears, already missing the comfort of Demetrius' arms and the reassurance of his words. Vision clearer, I watched as Aegeus removed his necklace and placed it in the water.

"Aquarius, you are needed."

I stared at him, my heart racing.

"Just wait, Aquaria. He will come."

I turned and stared out at the water, waiting for what seemed like forever, and then ripples appeared. I felt dizzy and light as the air. I was going to finally meet my father.

"Aquaria," he said as he walked out of the lapping waves. "Why have I been summoned? You know we are not supposed to meet until the Ascension."

My face crumbled and tears flowed freely as I dropped to the ground.

"You found out." It was a statement, not a question.

"How could I not? I'm horrible at Cup Carrying," I sobbed at the ground, tasting my salty tears.

"Ahh, but you are very accomplished at fighting, are you not?"

My head whipped up to stare at my father, a swelling of pride coming up despite my sadness. "You've seen me fight?"

He nodded. "I've watched you move up the ranks over the years. You fight like no other here."

"Then you have seen me fail over and over again, Father. What should I do? I cannot be a Cup Carrier for the Gods. I would be an embarrassment!"

My father looked grave. "You must, Aquaria. It was the only way I could secure your safety, and I had to fight to make it happen. You must."

"Perhaps there is another path for me, in the mortal wor—"

"No!" He strode forward and rested his hands on my shoulders. "If you do not ascend, Aquaria, you will become mortal. You would never see your brother or me again, nor experience the wonders of the Gods. No, you must be a Cup Carrier."

I took a deep breath. I knew this, I had been warned about it every year of my training. I'd thought about it often. A mortal life with Demetrius, or immortality with the Gods. With my family.

"You must keep trying, Aquaria. Keep persevering. I know you can. Take your fighting skills and transform them into those you need to be a Cup Carrier. You can do it."

I nodded. I did not want to disappoint my father. "I will try, I promise."

"Excellent." He stepped away and smiled gently. "I must go. I have my own duties to fulfil."

My smile fell from my face. I might never see him again. I leapt forward and hugged him close, until I could feel the steady beat of his heart. Mine swelled as he pulled me in tighter.

"I love you, Father."

"And I you, Aquaria. I cannot wait until we are reunited as a family."

"Aquaria, please, I love you."

My heart broke into song in my chest. It was the first time he'd declared it so openly. "I love you too, Demetrius. But it is a big thing you are asking of me."

"To choose, I know. I know it's selfish. I know you'll never see Aquaries or your father again or be with the Gods. But I want you to come with me. I want us to be together. You're happier with me, I see your troubles melt away every time we meet."

I looked into Demetrius' eyes and wondered how I could possibly choose between him, my soulmate, and my family. The Gods mattered little to me, but my father . . . my brother . . .

His tear-stained face destroyed my resolve. I pulled Demetrius close and pressed my lips softly into his, gently brushing the tears from his cheeks. His strong arms circled my back and pulled me closer. Our two hearts beating as one. How could I give this up?

The Ascension began. My toes wiggled in my sandals as my hair flew in the wind, whipping to the east, to where Demetrius waited by the water. I took a step closer. It was almost my turn. I looked to Zeus, and back to Aquaries. My stomach felt as though it was full of butterflies trapped in a windstorm. Another step. I looked to the east. Another step. I was running out of time. Aegeus was watching me, shaking his head. My throat tightened. I needed to go. I couldn't give Demetrius up forever, not for a job I was never meant to have. I mouthed a sorry at Aegeus, who closed his eyes. It looked like sadness, like regret. Would he give me a chance to escape? As my brother began his next step, I grabbed his arm. He turned and looked at me, saw the tears streaming down my face.

"No, Aquaria," he whispered.

"I love you, brother. Give my love to our father."

A tear fell from his eye as I kissed his cheek. I didn't look back at Zeus. I ran, fast. I pushed myself until the air coming from my lungs felt as though it was trying to squeeze through a tiny seashell. I barely felt my feet touch the earth. I made it to the edge of the Ascension grounds before I heard Aegeus bellow to Orien. I hoped Demetrius had the boat ready.

The thud of Orien's pursuit was behind me, his feet falling with heavy slaps on the debris of the forest. I jumped, clearing the stream, and grasped the lowest tree branch. I pulled myself up with an ease learned from years of practise. I was always quicker in the trees. I jumped from branch to branch. My breath was so loud that I couldn't hear if Orien was close. I was nearing the edge of the tree line, the pier in view. I smiled, Demetrius had the boat ready, he'd begun to loosen the ties. I cleared the last tree and looked back. Orien was close, too close.

"Move the boat, Demetrius!" I screamed.

"Watch out!" Demetrius yelled.

Orien shoved into me. I hit the ground hard but rolled and turned to face him. He steadied himself. A knife in his hand, a hard look on his face. I huffed, trying to catch my breath as I pulled my own knife from the sheath in my belt.

"Come back to camp, Aquaria. Do not make me do this."

"You know I am not meant for that life, Orien," I panted. "How many times did you laugh watching me try to carry the cup like my brother?"

"It does not matter. You must return. It is your destiny."

I shook my head, assessing Orien's wide stance. I moved swiftly to the left as he lunged and swiped my knife along his right arm. A scratch. I didn't want to hurt him either, though I couldn't see how I could avoid it. Not if I wanted to reach the boat. It was already beginning to drift. I took a step back towards it, but Orien moved with me. I felt his warm breath on me at the same time as the sharp sting of his blade tore through my left arm. He began to circle. I noticed a rock beneath the sand. Careful not to stare, I took another step. When Orien took his next, I charged straight at him. His ankle caught on the rock and he flew back into the sand. I rolled and landed on my feet once more and ran. I wouldn't get another chance. I didn't turn or slow this time.

My feet thudded on the pier as I got closer. I was going to have to jump.

Orien was chasing me, gaining on me. I was at the end. I closed my eyes and flung my body from the pier to the flat end of the boat. To Demetrius. My shoulder felt as though it had been zapped by one of Zeus' bolts. I leant heavily on the deck and looked to see the knife in my shoulder. The heat, the pain, it was agony. But Orien never missed a throw, I'd been stuck with him for punishments enough times to know. My heart almost stopped at the thought and I looked back at him, seeing the regret on his face. The blood rushed from my head as I turned to look at Demetrius. No!

I staggered to my feet, the searing pain in my shoulder becoming a dull ache in the back of my mind. I dropped to my knees beside Demetrius. Orien's other knife was hilt-deep in his stomach. There was blood pooling beneath him, barely any colour left in his face.

"Demetrius," I yelled, shaking his shoulders. "Answer me!"

His eyes fluttered open and my favourite smile touched his lips. He mumbled something but I couldn't hear. I leant closer. "Love you . . . Sorry."

"No! Demetrius you can't leave me!" I turned back to the shore, but Orien was gone. His job was done. My breathing was quick and shallow. I felt dizzy. What could I do? I looked around frantically. Nothing on board would help. The water! I needed something of the Realm. The knife. I screamed as I ripped it free from my shoulder. I staggered to the edge of the boat, then leant down and dipped the knife in.

"Father, please. I need you."

Demetrius lay on the deck as though he was dead. He couldn't be. I would save him. Where was my father? Where were the ripples? I turned back to Demetrius again and saw my father on the deck. "Father! Please help him!"

My father looked at me, grief clear in his eyes. I shook my head. "It's not too late, Father. Help him."

"He is almost gone Aquaria, even I cannot save him without cost." He shook his head and exhaled. "What would you give, daughter of mine, to save this human's life?"

I felt a glimmer of hope in my heart. "Anything, Father. Anything to save him, he is my soulmate."

"So be it, daughter. To save him will cost you your memories. Those of your own life, those of your life together." His voice broke. "Those of your family. You will never know us, or him. He will live, but he will also not remember."

I nodded my assent, and watched through eyes blurred with unshed tears, as my father drew the water from the ocean. It wrapped around Demetrius, lifting him from the boat before it wrapped me up in its cool, calm embrace.

My father walked to me through the water and pulled me close. "You have always been a true gift to me, and I will never forget you. Your brother will make a fine Cup Carrier to the Gods, but you my darling, will make a strong young woman." He leaned back, and looked into my eyes, that I realised matched his own. "I love you, daughter."

My tears streamed down my face. This cost was almost too much to bear. "I love you, Father."

He kissed my cheek softly, like the tide of the ocean lovingly caressing the sand on a calm summer's day, then he stepped back. The last things I saw were my soulmate, healed, and the love in my father's eyes.

"Aquaries, bring me more Ambrosia." Hera watched with amusement as he tore his eyes away from her Orb, clearly trying to hide what he'd been doing.

Aquaries walked gracefully towards her and poured the Ambrosia, just a light pinkness in his cheeks betraying his apparent calm. Hera pursed her lips for effect, causing him to hastily bow and move back to his position. She could tell his mistress had trained him well by the way he stood at attention and in the right light to accentuate his muscles. Hera couldn't help the slight pull to her lips as she saw him discreetly whisper a word of power to make her Orb zoom in on the scene he was watching. She'd had Picea, the Messenger, show him how to do it so that he would not suspect that Hera knew what he was looking at.

"Hera, why do you indulge him so?" Hebe muttered discreetly.

She turned to look at her daughter and paused her answer when Eileithyia spoke.

"Oh honestly, Hebe, it's been seven years since he lost his sister, and she has just had a baby. Why would he not want to know they are all okay?"

Hera nodded at the wiser of her two daughters before speaking her part. "It was not his choice to lose his sister, but lose her he did. It costs me nothing to ensure he has a little more light in his life. And besides, I want to know what she calls the girl."

The shock on Hebe's face was almost comical. "How do you know it is a girl?"

"I asked the Oracle, of course. Now be silent, I would like to listen in."

Hera ignored Hebe's childish eye roll and focused.

"What will we name her, honey?"

I kept looking at my little angel, my grin almost hurting my face since it'd been there so long. Her eyes were like mine, the beautiful blue of the ocean, I loved them. I shook my head a little and focussed on my husband's question and the name I had in mind. It was a strange one by today's standards. I didn't know why, but I felt drawn to it, like there was some sort of underlying connection. Which I suppose would seem more insane if I could've actually remembered anything before I had turned twenty-one, but for all I knew I grew up in the middle of an ocean. Either way, I hoped he wouldn't veto it.

"Honey?"

I'd taken too long to answer. I smiled at him, a little embarrassed. "Sorry sweetie, I was just thinking about the name. I know it's a little different, but I'd like to call her Aquaria?"

A strange look crossed his face, but before I could ask, he answered me.

"It's perfect."

About the Author:

Shay Laurent has loved reading and writing since her youth. She was born in Dubbo NSW and has since moved to Western Sydney. She lives with her husband and two young daughters. When she's not with her daughters playing peekaboo or reading their favourite books, she's dreaming up imaginary worlds and committing them to paper.

Shay mostly writes tales of fantasy and she is publishing her debut novel, a Young Adult epic fantasy in 2020. She also loves to connect with readers and writers around the world. You will often find her on Twitter @slaurentauthor.

To find out more about Shay, you can check out her website: www.shaylaurent.com

WATERBORNE

DL Fleming

Danny Bell lifted the heavy frame of the diving gear onto his shoulders and strapped the belt closed around his hips. The rain had kept him on land for three days, acid from the skies mixing with river water and stirring up the heavy salts that usually sank to the bottom.

"Need some help, boy?" The words were pleasant enough but Danny steeled himself to turn and meet the sneer in Kruger's bright blue eyes.

Behind Kruger a line of rundown shacks straggled alongside the river. Patches of rust the colour of old blood and white crusts of salt streaked the wooden planks, stray chunks of brick and sheets of corrugated iron. The shacks were surrounded by food scraps and piles of twice-discarded junk: decaying plastic bags, broken chairs, mouldy clothes with threads unravelling.

Small communities of scavengers came and went, fossicking among the wreckage and then moving on, their energy leached away in the unrelenting abrasion of the salty water.

Danny had lived here all his life, in the house his parents built. It was one of the few shelters that were more than a lean-to, with three small rooms and a narrow verandah out the front.

Most of the old city was underwater, along with its treasures. He had travelled once with his father three days walk to the south and had seen where it had blown its banks to become a wide delta clogged with mud as it emptied into the super saline sea. Nothing can live in there, his father had said, the salt levels had risen too quickly for the sea animals to adapt. The water of the inland rivers was still capable of sustaining shoals of small fish, but anything larger than the width of a hand was rare.

Which is why Danny and his older sister Lisette had continued the underwater salvage missions after their parents died. Danny had learned from his father how to handle the diving gear, and despite his overblown boasting, in Kruger's hands the equipment would be ruined within the day. Everyone knew it. That didn't mean Kruger liked to admit it.

Danny looked Kruger in the eye as he finished buckling the straps for the air tanks, planted his feet wide to spread the weight and straightened his shoulders. On land the diving suit was heavy and awkward, and one push could send him sprawling, helpless as an upturned-bug, until he could unstrap it all again.

"No thanks, all done." *As you can see, asshole.*

Danny plodded towards the end of the floating jetty he'd lashed together from thick beams of wood and short steel joists floating on plastic barrels and empty metal kegs. He knew Kruger wouldn't follow. If Danny tipped into the water, his face would suffer, with the mask not yet in place, but he'd survive. Kruger wouldn't.

At the end of the jetty he put the breathing tube into his mouth and closed the faceplate, sealing his breath inside the system.

The salvage from the city couldn't last forever, and some people were learning to harvest the plants that had been able to adapt to the new environment on land. His mother had taught him that a similar change would be taking place in the water. There were tiny, unseen creatures that were the beginning of a food chain, from which larger and more varied life could grow.

His parents had argued often in a friendly way about what might be happening down there, something they called radical mutation. His father said definitely not, nature just didn't work that way; his mother preferred maybe: maybe such a complete change in conditions could lead to an unexpected result.

But to have any kind of a future, they needed to find new ways of getting fresh water.

Like the boxes he had rigged up last year to see if the process of heating and cooling by the sun would un-salt the river water. Danny felt the slow burn of anger as he recalled finding the boxes in pieces. There was no way to prove who was responsible, but he knew it must have been deliberate. He had expected the reflective surface of the salvaged metal plates would corrode, but the frames should have been strong enough, they shouldn't have collapsed like that after just one week. *One successful week*, he reminded himself. He had been able to collect enough water—brackish but drinkable—for a whole family's weekly ration. *If each family had three or four of them . . .*

Without warning, the planks beneath Danny's feet wobbled violently and he staggered, trying to regain his balance.

"Still holding up okay I see!" Kruger grinned, with one foot resting on the ground and the other on the jetty where he'd stamped it down.

Come over here and say that, Danny thought. *Please, just step out onto the jetty.* He bent his knees, jumped as high as he could and twisted sideways. The floating structure sprang upward and then smacked back down with a boom. He surfaced and looked back.

Kruger had leaped away from the water. He glared at Danny with a mixed expression of fury and fear.

Danny smiled.

The outer layer of the suit quickly absorbed water and the fibres swelled to create a barrier which kept the inner layer dry and protected his skin. Danny was free to sink under the surface into the quiet world of the river. No one down there to bother him, just his own graceful movements.

When he came up to the surface again, the settlement was no longer in sight. He kicked along slowly, noting the changing colour of the short grasses which poked up on the land. The fresh mud on the riverbank shone wetly brown in the sunlight, with a sheen like mucus and a thin shimmer of rising steam. The tiny mosses and fungal blooms that gathered every dry season were starting to shrivel. They wouldn't survive the rainy season, but their little life, their potential, lived on in the seeds left behind after their brief flowering.

It was taking him longer to reach the unsearched areas. There would come a time when his supply of air wouldn't be enough to take him there and back in a day and he would have to think about recruiting someone to help him carry the equipment over land. Bevin perhaps. At sixteen, he was three years younger than Danny, and strong enough physically. His mother Joan was one of the few adults who wanted to learn the things Danny's parents had passed on.

It had been so much easier when Lisette was here. He didn't think *when she had still been alive*, couldn't really believe that she was dead. Some mornings he woke with the sensation that she was just in the other room, or sitting on the stump outside the door where she liked to collect the morning sunlight on her face, and surely any moment she would walk in and bang on the doorframe to rouse her sleepyhead brother out of bed.

She had been following him on land the day she went missing; there when he dived down, and then not, when he resurfaced. He had dragged himself over to the bank, but the suit was too awkward on land. All he had been able to do was remove his face mask and call until his voice became a croak. Then he'd left one precious spear dug upright in the bank as a marker and struggled his way back to the settlement, weary and desolate.

They had looked for her for a week.

Kruger had surprised him by helping to organise the search, although after the incident with the boxes, Danny wondered how sincere the effort had been.

He noted the position of the sun and picked up his pace, kicking with his flippers until he came to the place he had left his marker floats three days ago, where a section of the riverbank had fallen away to reveal a deep side channel that might offer a regular yield.

Each of the floats was connected to a haulage crate hanging a metre or so below the surface, and Danny carefully strung the five crates together with a second, thinner line that he attached to his belt. That safety line was vital—it was easy to get lost down there, following twists and turns in the dark. Once his preparations were complete, he dove under the surface again and kicked away from the sky.

Danny wondered if he would see any bodies.

They could still spook him, the pale drifters, garments shredding to rags around them and trailing like tentacles. Their bodies were grub-fat with peeling skin bloated by the absorption of water and wrinkled into unusual contours by the saltiness. Pickled walnuts in a jar, his father had joked. Of course, he'd laughed because his father did, but had not understood. What were walnuts?

Most of the bodies had been washed out to sea long ago, but sometimes he came across some that had been confined inside the spaces of a building, suspended in slow decay as if waiting. His movements through the water would make them bob and spin in a silent parody of a dance.

The ones with long dark hair were the worst. In Danny's nightmares the hair would wash aside like water weed and he would see Lisette's big brown eyes peering out of a distorted, ugly face.

He reached the top of a submerged building. This was the best part of the whole job: exploring a new area with the promise of new supplies.

There was enough light for him to search through a couple of floors and scope the layout, note the location of cupboards and other storage areas and, most importantly, the plumbing system. Often the pipes had buckled and broken, and the metal was still useful if it could be dislodged and taken back to the settlement. But sometimes the plumbing contained fresh water that had been in the pipes when the floodwaters came. On two rare, miraculous occasions he and his father had found a building with the plumbing still connected, far down in the deep, to an underground reservoir.

The first priority would be to take samples from this top floor before scoping out the next level. There was plenty of time to explore whatever bounty this wreck might contain. Be methodical, his father had always said. Get all the most accessible supplies before going for a prize which might use up more energy to obtain than it provided. Focus on the known benefit, before chasing a dream.

Danny glided through the rooms and corridors, avoiding the stairways and the inky, four-sided fissures that descended into the building, which his father had called elevator shafts.

He swam through an opening on the other side and turned to look back at the structure. There was a cloudiness in the water that shouldn't be there, more than his movements should have caused. The water below was too dark to see the bottom of the building and it was deeper here than on the other side of the channel. As he swam out over the blackness of the drop-off to investigate, he noticed. It was much colder too.

Doubt bloomed in his stomach. Sometimes there were patches where the water was more acid than others. If that was the case, he would have to clear this site much quicker than he had planned.

As he reached for the string of sample bottles hooked to his belt, he felt a ripple underneath him. He froze in place, flippers paddling just enough to keep him upright. It had felt like an earth tremor; a swish, a wash, of movement below. He caught a glimpse of something coming up from the deep on his right, between him and the building. A dark shadow which grew paler as it rose.

Must be a body down there.

Then he realised with a thump in his chest that it was moving too fast to be floating. Kicking his flippers hard, he struck out towards the building. Whatever it was, it was bigger than a person. Blood thumped in his eardrums.

The huge creature swept up alongside the building then breached the surface to breathe. It was twice his length and wide, round at the belly, with a tapering tail.

He followed it upwards.

In the light he saw the sheen of its skin. Beautiful, flowing colours. Silvery blue, a pink as pale and soft as the sky before dawn and a streak of orange that flashed like a stirred ember in the murky water.

Danny kicked his own flippers softly, trying not to frighten it off. Such a large creature—was it a fish, or mammal? He thought its skin looked smooth, not scaly like the fish that swam inland: little gems darting through the rivers, moving flowers in the deep.

The creature circled him in a graceful arc. At the end of the tail was a little split that divided it into two sections, each with a sort of fringe of smaller divisions. Danny counted five on each side. Its flippers were flat and wide to propel it through the water, and these too had a fringed edge, so they looked like thin fingers. Wondering if it was aware of his presence, he stretched out his hand slowly.

With a flick of its tail it moved toward the surface again, this time cresting directly over his head. He craned his neck in wonder to gaze at its pale green underside, which was thick but perfectly smooth, without a callus or a bump. *Definitely skin. It's a mammal.*

Then, as quickly as it had come, the creature dove back into blackness and was gone. Danny trod water for a few minutes, hoping, but it didn't return.

Finally, he went up to the surface, loosened his faceplate and removed the breathing tube so he could grin and laugh. He had to let out the excitement that fizzed in his veins. There was life in these waters! Amazing. There must be a whole ecosystem down there, to support a creature that big. Something new, adapted to the increased salt in the water. His mind shied away from the image of the drifters as he wondered what it could possibly find to eat down below.

The sun had moved past midday. *Time for work*, he told himself. *Maybe I'll see it again tomorrow.*

Danny arrived back at the settlement near dusk. He had taken samples from three taps on the top floor and noted the location of several large cupboards and storage lockers.

Since the rooms looked like they had once been part of a housing complex, there may not be much equipment, but there were metal fixtures and some large sheets of unbroken glass in the internal doors. He could use all of that. He hummed to himself, feeling good about the find and the sighting of the incredible animal. He poked his head out of the water and rested his elbows on the end of the jetty, enjoying the sunset and the sensation of weightlessness for a few moments before he struggled up onto land in the waterlogged suit.

Kruger and a few other men were walking down to the water's edge. A band of the older children ran behind them. Everyone's faces suddenly became very animated and they pointed at the water. The children jumped up and down.

Danny took off his mask. He could hear them shouting and turned toward the direction they were pointing in time to see the end of a large tail disappearing.

Kruger and the other men started running to the gantry near the jetty that they used to haul the larger salvage onto land. Kruger shouted something and two of the men peeled off to head up the shore to Danny's shack.

"Hey!" Danny shouted but they continued to rummage among the equipment he stored on the outside wall under a small overhang. They grabbed a large net and began carrying it down to the water.

He hauled himself onto the jetty and tried to get his fumbling fingers to unbuckle the straps of his air tanks. Dragging them behind him, he shouted out again to the men gathered near the gantry.

"What are you doing with my nets?"

Kruger spared him a brief, triumphant glance. "You brought home the jackpot this time boy," he crowed.

"What do you mean?"

"There's enough meat on that thing to feed us for a week!"

The bottom fell out of Danny's stomach. They couldn't be serious.

"But we don't know anything about it. It could be a totally new species, maybe part of a breeding pair . . ." His words trailed away as he saw that none of them were listening. Some of the women had come to see what the fuss was about, summoned by their excited children. They gasped in awe as the creature breached the surface again, breathing a spray of water over its body.

Joan folded her arms across her chest. "He has a point," she said to Kruger. "How can you even be sure it's edible?"

Kruger grunted. "Why wouldn't it be?"

"Maybe we should study it for a while."

"It will be gone by the time 'study' it," Kruger scoffed. "We need meat now."

The men had attached the net to the gantry and begun swinging it out over the water. One of them turned to look at Danny. "How we gonna lure it in? Any idea what it eats?"

Danny felt disgusted. He shook his head. "There's nothing to eat out there but the small fry."

"Maybe there's a whole bunch of them. Maybe Bell boy's been keeping it a secret," Kruger accused.

The comment made no sense, but Danny was too exhausted to challenge it. The weight of the air tanks was making his arm numb. "Today's the first time I've seen anything like that."

"We only have your word for that, don't we?"

One of the men lowering the net waved his arm. "It's coming closer."

"Looks like it followed Bell home," Kruger said. "Maybe it wants to make friends with him."

The men near Kruger started to close in on Danny. He wanted to jump out of the way but he was hampered by the heavy diving suit. A hand gripped his shoulder as a loud shout came from the men at the gantry. The arm of it bent under the pull of a sudden weight in the net. Danny was shoved hard sideways and sprawled on the ground.

He watched the net rise high into the air then swing round ready to dump the creature onto the bank. Everyone jumped back to avoid the acid splash of river water. A puddle of it formed around Danny's legs but the suit protected him.

"Hand me a knife," Kruger ordered.

The creature hung quietly above him in the net, the colours of its skin muted out here in the air, though the flash of orange under its throat was still brilliant.

He rose slowly until he stood facing it, eyeing the pointed beak of its mouth. Then the eyes opened and he staggered in shock, an inarticulate noise escaping from his throat. His nightmare from the deep was coming true in this gigantic, monstrous form. The eyes were huge—at least twice the size of a human's—but the colour and the shape and most especially the expression were unmistakably Lisette. The creature gazed back at him calmly. One eye winked.

An onlooker passed Kruger a knife with a thin, curved blade designed for skinning hides.

"No!" Danny's mouth was too dry to give the word much force.

The men moved in, eager to witness the kill.

Kruger raised his right hand, lifting the blade high. Danny tensed, summoning his waning strength to step forward and knock him aside.

A luminescent mucus shimmered on the creature's skin and Danny saw the pointed beak opening wide. The tail slapped down and the round belly humped upward, the giant creature lunged forward. The beak closed with a snap around Kruger's arm. The knife fell to the ground.

Everyone shouted as the animal tossed Kruger's body high into the air and humped back towards the water.

A stream of crimson sprayed from the wound.

The men nearest the river tried to leap out of the way but one swipe of the tail knocked two down and another three were barrelled into the water.

Women screamed and children raced in panic. Then the animal was over the edge and into the river. The five men in the water splashed frantically and screamed in pain, but no one wanted to risk their own skin to save them. After a brief time, their movements stilled and the six bodies floated face down.

Ignoring the uproar and heedless of his air tanks abandoned on the riverbank, Danny stumbled up to his shack. Once inside he closed the door tight behind him and leaned on it, letting the wood keep him upright despite the uncontrollable trembling in his legs. He had seen the smile of satisfaction in the eyes—Lisette's eyes—as she slid into the water.

Danny watched Joan approaching up the slope to his shack, where he sat listlessly watching the slow swell and flow of the river. The water was running white again now the rains had returned.

"Morning Danny." Joan stepped onto the verandah. She folded her arms across her chest and fixed him with an even gaze.

"Morning," he said mildly. "How's Bevin?"

"He's fine," she replied. "What about you? When you going out again?"

He shrugged. "Not sure. Not so much need now, is there?" He pitched his head in a dip towards the side of his shack, where the new un-salting boxes sat in rows.

"It's not just about the water though. There's other things we need down there."

"We can make do for a while longer with the stuff we have." Danny's mouth tightened into a firm line. The dwindling settlement had survived through the winter by cannibalising the belongings abandoned by those who fled following Kruger's death. More would leave now the weather was warming up.

He knew he should move on too, establish a settlement further down the river near the new site. Although he'd resisted training a new partner when Lisette first disappeared, over the winter he had been teaching Bevin how to dive. It had been going well. Bevin paid attention and he learnt quickly. Danny was sure he and Joan would help him build a new jetty.

It was a year since Lisette disappeared, six months since Kruger and the others had gone down into the deep.

Autumn and winter had been a long file of days in which he slept, first twelve, then fourteen, then sixteen or more hours at a stretch.

His waking hours were filled with trying to forget.

He couldn't think of it as Lisette, couldn't accept the idea that she could have been so radically transformed, so quickly.

But the memory of those eyes wouldn't leave him. They had been large and deep brown like hers and the shock of recognition he felt had been real. It was not just a physical resemblance; it was the fact she had looked back at him that he could not deny.

It took all his courage to make a dive. Some days he thought he caught a glimpse of a long pale shape moving through the water, a ripple or a dapple of light reflected by the breeze ruffling the surface, and he couldn't re-enter the water for a week. He didn't want to take a chance on meeting it—her—again in the deep.

"Weather's fine today," Joan said. "If you're not going out, would you let Bevin use the gear?"

The timbers of the shack were warm against Danny's back. Joan was right. The weather was good and it had been a while. The air was heavy, building up for the spring rain, and he felt the same kind of restless pressure building inside.

"Sure, I'll take him out." Danny got up from his comfortable slump and stretched. His shoulder creaked. Really, it had been too long, his muscles could do with the workout. "I'll go check the lines, send Bevin along and I'll mark him out to the site."

Joan nodded and gave him a smile of encouragement.

The trip to the site was uneventful. Bevin had marked his previous exploration using a line tied with yellow strips of plastic descending into the darker water. Danny was content to sit on the shore enjoying the sunshine and passing equipment to Bevin in the water. He'd found a metal doorframe and brought it to the surface so Danny could haul it out with a rope. Danny enjoyed the feel of his muscles working. His spare suit was in the trolley with the rest of their gear, and he played with the idea of pulling it on for a quick dip in the river. In spite of everything, the water called to him.

He sighed. *Enough for today. Better save my strength for the journey home.* He signalled with his thumb and Bevin nodded and began kicking his way to the shore.

When Bevin removed his mask, Danny smiled. "Nothing fancy, but that's good, solid building material," he said.

Bevin smiled back at him, a shy pride spreading over his face.

The sluggish feeling that engulfed Danny faded for the first time in months. The sense of satisfaction he felt from a solid day's work had lifted his mood. For a moment the small plants along the western edge of the river blazed with a deep orange reflected from the rays of the setting sun. Each tiny leaf glowed, as if a thousand candles had been set into the riverbank. Danny breathed in softly. It was beautiful.

Ripples appeared between the shore and where Bevin was treading water. Danny's heart thumped. "Put your mask back on," he said roughly.

Bevin looked around in confusion.

They broke surface, six of the creatures, smaller than Lisette and with different colourings but the same kind of mutation. One of them tossed the body of a drifter into the air with its beaky snout and crunched an arm off the pickled corpse. The creature turned to him and blinked its bright, bright blue eyes.

Danny jumped up from where he was crouched at the water's edge and the rope snaked away into the water as the doorframe sank. He shouted in alarm as a huge shape shot up out of the river and barrelled into him. He overbalanced and tipped forward into the water. Although he knew it was pointless, he screwed his eyes shut tight against the sting of the acid.

Something brushed against his leg and his eyes sprang open. His skin was on fire. He struggled and thrashed, kicking out as hard as he could toward the shore, but the water seemed unbearably thick and syrupy.

Then there she was, Lisette, her strange beak smiling at him and her gaze full of understanding. The sense of loss he had felt since she disappeared, the effort of refusing to accept what she had become, welled up in him and he let out an anguished cry.

And stopped struggling. Let the acid burn it all away. She laid her broad forehead against his brow and cradled him within the warmth of her soft belly as they drifted, gliding gently into the current.

About the Author:

DL Fleming is a writer based in Canberra, Australia. She holds Bachelor and Masters degrees in communications and creative writing, and in 2018 she received a place in the ACT Writers Centre's HARDCOPY program for emerging writers (fiction). DL Fleming is currently working on her first full-length manuscript, a work of young teen speculative fiction about nanotechnology. Two of her flash fiction stories are included in the anthology IMPACT! Stories that Pack a Punch, *released in April 2019.*

THE WATER BEARER

Dee Cheers

On the edge of the Sand Sea, the city of faux mudbrick writhed in the haze of the mid-morning heat. The towering buildings, pierced here and there with small high windows, and low doors, presented an almost blank face to the glaring light of the smaller sun. It could be any ancient city, on any number of worlds, were it not for the clutter of comms towers and dishes encrusting every roof.

In the walled courtyard of the caravanserai, Zaidel slumped back into his chair, tossing his sheet onto the table in frustration. The sprinkling of fallen petals from the spreading atoria tree above him scattered under the impact.

"Twelve weeks," he muttered to the empty garden. "Not nearly enough time." To the south, the super-giant the natives called the Fat One lurked behind the towering mountain range. Each day the tendrils of its malevolent heat flickered higher above the rim, signalling the beginning of summer, and an end to the caravans for the season.

Zaidel reached into the cooler beside his chair and extracted another bottle. He popped the top, threw the small plastic lid into the overgrown garden bed, and downed half of the ice-cold liquid in one long swallow.

Barely three hours after dawn, and it was already scorching. Sweat beaded across his forehead, burned a deep brown by months out in the sun, and his shirt clung to him in wet, rank patches.

He could go inside, into the icy cold of air-conditioned offices, but he preferred the quiet heat of the garden to frigid corridors filled with the chatter of colony administration. He downed the rest of the beer, and let the bottle slip from his fingers, to clink and rattle into the leaf litter with the other empties. Zaidel closed his eyes, and let the alcohol take him.

"Lord?" the squeaky voice dragged him from his doze. In front of the table stood one of the natives, a small one by the look of it, its grey-green fingers twisting with nervousness.

"Where did you come from?" he demanded, trying to project some semblance of authority. Great. It was not even lunchtime, and one of the damned frogs had found him passed out.

The little native took a step backwards, flinching at Zaidel's raised voice. "I am here, lord. To be a bearer. For your caravan." Little hisses punctuated each syllable as it struggled to use Standard.

"Those inside," it waved towards the colony office, "they said you were hiring."

Zaidel leaned forward and looked the native up and down. "A bearer? How old are you?" he asked. "Ten?"

"Thirteen, lord." The nictitating membranes of its eyes flicked in and out, betraying its fear. "Old enough. Yes?"

Thirteen. That made it nearly sixteen in standard years. Still not an adult, but he'd heard the military were taking recruits that young now, the losses were that high.

"It's Zaidel," he snapped. "Not this lord nonsense."

The alien flinched again. "Forgiveness lo—Zaidel. I wish to be bearer. I can carry twenty, easily. Five trips." It held up a small grey hand, wriggling its fingers in confirmation.

Despite the mangled speech, Zaidel could hear the desperation in its voice. It must come from a small burrow, to be asking for this.

"So, how many in your burrow?" Zaidel didn't want to know the answer and it came out as anger.

The alien reacted as if struck, but held its ground. "There are four little ones below me. One old. Other old was bearer. Six trips he did, carried thirty," it replied, its hissy, squeaky voice full of pride.

Four. Zaidel's stomach knotted. It wasn't unknown for whole burrows to die from lack of food and water during the long summer sequestered underground. The small ones, the children, were particularly vulnerable. He rubbed his hand through his hair in frustration. He needed bearers, but not children. Had the war effort come to this, that they would sacrifice children as well? Perhaps this one wouldn't be suitable, and he could send it on its way with a clear conscience.

"Let me see," he said, gesturing to it to lift the grubby rags clothing its frame. It closed its eyes and slowly raised the ragged tunic, displaying the thick grey-green hide, the heavy drapes of skin around the squat, reptilian body, the tell-tale line of bright yellow scales. Zaidel frowned. He wasn't supposed to take breeders; the colony administrators were concerned about the falling population. Not concerned enough though, to ensure they survived the summer.

"No," he said, shaking his head. "I can't take breeders; they'll revoke my license."

The alien gave a small wail. "Please lord. Please Zaidel." It held out its hands beseechingly. "Without this, all my burrow will die. The little ones will never see the cool time again," it pleaded. "Please."

Nausea roiled through him. This was wrong, but without the mineral mined in the desert sands, they couldn't make enough drives to power the battleships, scout ships and fighters needed to keep the invaders at bay.

"All right." He held up a hand. "Just wait." The usual rate was fifty stones. He did a quick calculation on the sheet, aware of the large, yellow eyes, with their flicking membrane, watching him. The figures stared back at him. Not enough, they'd all be dead weeks before autumn came. He should say no. Send it on its—no, her way. He wasn't the colony's conscience.

Or. He could take a smaller cut. This time. His passage back to the base world was already paid for. No home world reunion for him, that was long gone, swept away by the war over a decade ago. All of his pay would go on beer, whores and forgetting.

"All right," he said again. He had half a cooler left, enough to wash the bitterness out of his throat, once this was done. "Turn around."

The native girl turned and lifted its clothes once again so that Zaidel could mark its back with the caravan logo. "Be at the cisterns tomorrow, an hour before the Little One rises above the mountains," he ordered. "A hundred stones per run." His voice hardened. "But you'd better be able to do twenty or I won't pay at all. Understood?"

The girl smiled a great toothless rubbery grin, and bowed. "Thank you, Zaidel. Thank you. I can do twenty. And five trips. You will see."

The city of the Tall Ones loomed silent above her. Every doorway, every window, was shuttered and barred against the rising sun. Behind each one was food, and water and the artificial cold, enough for many, many Tall Ones. Just not enough for her people. Even the little dhoy, once an animal of open fields, had been reduced to scavenging amongst the remains of the market, seeking whatever shade they could squeeze into.

Grenix put these thoughts away and hurried along the street, keeping to the shadows. It did no good to dwell on what might have been. Overhead, the shade sails strung across the passages barely moved in the oppressive morning air. The sigil on her back weighed on her, like a collapsed burrow. The Fat One approached, and with it the time of sorrows. Not this year, she reminded herself. This summer, the little ones would all survive to breathe the cool autumn air.

The burrows were on the outskirts of the city, in the low hills and ridges that stretched up to the walls of the mountains. Once, a long time ago, her people had occupied the area where the city of the tall ones now stood. The burrows, their entrances protected by the thick walls of the mudbrick buildings, extended down into the dark, cool bedrock. Underground, supplies were hoarded for the summer and the deep, cold cisterns held enough water to support a population of millions. A simple, pre-technological society, of farmers, craftsmen and wise old ones. Until the Tall Ones came in great noisy ships, their hands full of gifts and their words full of lies. The mudbrick buildings disappeared, replaced by something else, a pretend sort of mud, that smelled wrong and felt wrong, but that didn't matter because the tall ones lived in them now, and her people's burrows were pushed further and further out to the edge.

Out here, the heat from the Little One, the smaller of the two suns, beat down onto the dusty ground. Every footstep set off a puff of pale dust, until her legs and the hem of her tunic turned grey.

Grenix increased her pace. Thirst ate at her. There hadn't been enough water for everyone this morning. She'd managed to steal a few mouthfuls from the garden while the tall one slept. It had been warm and rank, but she had drunk far worse. Stealing water was the worst crime, even from the tall ones, who wasted it on fountains and gardens. She would remind mother to return a stone, as payment.

Finally, she reached her burrow. Grenix pushed the thick door covering aside and stepped into the small antechamber, grateful to be home.

Zaidel pulled the door closed and dropped his sheet onto the charging point. The lights flickered on and the air conditioning whirred to life. He leaned back against the door, regarding the room with disgust. The single bed, covered in a tangle of rumpled, unwashed bedding took up one wall. A small table sat between the bed and the wall, almost swamped in a mountain of empty bottles and food wrappers. The other wall, no more than a few steps away from the bed, held a desk, with a cooler underneath, partially buried under a pile of clothing, boots and more rubbish. A door led to a tiny bathroom. The underground room, with its lack of windows, felt like a cell. It stank of sweat, dirt, and stale booze. Zaidel sniffed at one rank underarm, cursed, and dragged off his boots and clothes, kicking them towards the rest of the clutter.

The body monitor on his wrist started beeping. "Fucking bureaucracy," he snarled. "All right, I'm fucking drinking water."

He kicked enough of the pile away from the cooler so he could open the door and pulled out a bottle of water. The top landed into the same pile as the dirty clothes, and he drank until the beeping stopped.

He leant into the bathroom to empty the rest into the small sink, when he stopped and held the bottle up to the light, sloshing the liquid back and forth. Probably about two hundred mils of water, he estimated. Worth about ten stones on the black market. Enough to keep a small one alive for a day, maybe. He stared at it for a moment, then bent down and rummaged through the clothes until he found the lid and returned the bottle to the cooler. Zaidel dropped down onto the bed, trying to forget large yellow eyes, pleading for her family's life.

Deep within the cool bedrock, Grenix pattered along the burrow passage and into the main chamber. The four little ones rolled and tumbled on the rugs in some game of their own devising that entailed them piling on top of each other, squealing and shrieking. Grenix swooped down and picked up the littlest one from the heap of flailing arms and legs and carried her down to the eating area. Mother stood in front of the bench, stirring a pot over a single heater element.

"What's for dinner?" she asked.

Mother turned and smiled. "I managed to get a small bag of chacco root and some water. It's not much, but we will all eat tonight." Her smile slipped a little and Grenix could see the fear underneath. The glutinous mass of cooked chacco would fill bellies, but offer no nutritional value. The little ones needed real food to grow.

"It's all right," Grenix said, "you will have food and water tomorrow, and enough for summer. This one," she bounced the baby on her hip, "will have a name come the cooltime."

On her mother's face confusion gave way to terrible understanding, and she let out a small wail of grief. "No, please, don't tell me you signed on as a bearer."

Grenix lowered the little one to the floor and hugged her mother. "It's the only thing left," she said. "I can do five trips, and they will pay one hundred stones a trip. More than enough to keep you alive, and all the little ones." She struggled to keep her voice full of confidence, despite the absolute terror boiling in her stomach.

"No," mother sobbed into her shoulder, "what will I do without you?"

"To be water bearer is a sacred duty, one our ancestors held as the highest honour. I can do this. And the tall ones will pay well," Grenix reassured her, trying not to cry.

"But when summer ends?" her mother asked, her voice broken with sobs, "what then?"

Grenix bent down and collected the nameless little one again. "Then perhaps," she said, her voice full of sudden, pitiless anger, "they will not return, or if we are blessed, their war will sweep them all away, and they will have no need for the desert mineral they so lust after."

Only an hour after dawn and it was already too warm outside. Once the supergiant Beta Aquarii peeked over the mountains, the surface temperature would be above the boiling point of water. The caravan crews would leave, fleeing to worlds much cooler, wetter, less unforgiving. Only the permanent colony staff would remain, retreating to the underground bunkers beneath the city, carved out of the remains of the native's primitive burrow system.

Down here, at the cisterns, the air was cool, full of moisture. Zaidel strode along the walkway, nodding to his men as they finished the clean-up. Along the edge of the cisterns, a long line of plastic tubs were filling quickly as the men shovelled in the last of the remains. The slabs of pinkish meat and white bones reached almost to the top of each container.

Zaidel frowned at one of the new men, Jern. He held a scrap of meat between his fingers, teasing a dhoy. The multi-legged animal leaped and chittered as it tried to reach the treat held just out of reach.

"Hey!" Zaidel yelled, full of anger, "stop fucking around and get this cleaned up. And have some fucking respect."

Jern scowled, but did as he was ordered, tossing the meat into the nearest tub, and kicking the vermin across the synthcrete pathway. It hit the wall, and lay there, jerking spasmodically.

Under the huge curving vault of the cistern tunnel, the line of vehicles and trailers stood in line, waiting for their crews.

"The new one," Zaidel asked a driver, "how much did it take?"

The driver consulted his sheet. "Twenty point five. I've loaded it into the last trailer." He pointed down the line of vehicles.

"Thanks." Zaidel moved down the line, checking the loads against his sheet, testing all the ties downs and hitches. It would take over a week, under the cloudless green-blue sky to cross the wasteland of the Sand Sea desert to the first mining camp. He couldn't afford any problems.

He climbed up into the lead vehicle and gave the signal to move out. The caravan of wide tyred vehicles and their line of trailers rumbled up the tunnel and through the city gates.

Vehicles after vehicle, each with its trailer packed full. The bladders of water, every green-grey hide painted with the company logo, sloshed with the movement.

About the Author:

Dee Cheers has been reading, watching and writing science fiction since childhood. Currently writing her first full-length novel, she describes writing as the most frustratingly rewarding thing she has ever done.

In real life, her work takes her to some of the most remote areas of Australia. Dee lives in Brisbane, with a dog and two cats.

THIS IS THE DAWNING (PART II)

Helena McAuley

Douglas Upton Day was probably not a name well thought out by his parents. Still, Doug endured it, just as he endured other things—long commuter rides with people packed in like sweaty sardines, book-to-film adaptations where they change the ending, rent for even a one-bedroom flat exploding to astronomical prices, baristas who couldn't get his order right a fundamental inability to woo women, and the constant teasing and taunting of his colleagues. Still, it wasn't all bad. Mi-goreng noodles were cheap, indie authors were on the rise, and the term 'comic book' was increasingly being replaced by 'graphic novel'.

He had his health. That, and a brand-new copy of *End of Fantasy XVII*. Keys already in the stuff-dish and bag in the hallway, Doug put a pot of water on to boil and prepared himself for a 4K, action–adventure, turn-based, steampunk-themed night of grinding.

The console bleeped to life and demanded input.

"Oh, yeah, baby," Doug muttered, lovingly inserting the disc. "You're gettin' a full workout tonight."

There was a knock at the door to his apartment. Strange, because he distinctly remembered closing the downstairs security door. *He's locking it up, and checking it twice!* was the usual mantra. Maybe it was the crazy neighbour from across the hall who only remembered your face if she needed something. Or maybe, it occurred to him as his hand hesitated on the latch, it was the fuzz, finally come to investigate his *'I acquired it perfectly legitimately'* blog-group.

It was times like this that he really wished he'd pressured the real estate into fixing the broken chain-lock. Or installing a spy hole.

He cracked the door open just enough to see through and set his foot firmly against the base of the door. The face that peered at him from beyond didn't look like police, but it certainly wasn't the crazy neighbour either. It was a tall, broad-shouldered guy with grey-streaked ash-blond hair and three-day growth. Eyes of grey that weren't entirely friendly fixed on him.

"Douglas."

"Err . . ." was all he could think to say.

"Let me in, we need to talk."

"Yeah," Doug drawled. "How about . . . No?" He closed and bolted the door, again wishing for a chain-lock, and took several steps back. His hand reached into his pocket for his phone, but the pocket was empty. He must've left it on the kitchen bench with the noodles.

The man banged on the door again. "This will be a lot easier if you just invite me in."

Invite him in? What was he, a vampire? In that case, double-no. What was best in this situation? A salt barrier? Holy water? Not that Doug made it a rule to keep holy water in the house, but he probably still had that bottle his mum brought back from Lourdes somewhere. And he only had minced garlic . . .

"Douglas," the man growled, his voice was laced with warning.

"Not a chance, Creepy McCreepFace," Doug shouted back, retreating further into the safety of the hallway. "If you want to talk to me, go downstairs and use the intercom. Otherwise, I'm calling the cops."

There was a stifled curse from the other side of the portal. "Have it your way."

The guy walked through the door. Not opening it, not breaking it, but *through it*—like it was nothing but air.

"Madre de Dios!" Doug stumbled over his feet in his haste to back up and fell sprawling to the floor. His blood ran cold, his heart threatening to tear itself from his chest.

The grey eyes seemed to look *through* him, as if he were as insubstantial as the door.

"Aquarius." The man towered over Doug as he spoke. "It's me, Capricorn. The Dawning is upon us. I need you to incarnate *now*."

Devil be cursed for fire-hazard, one-way-in one-way-out, second floor flats. But thank God for Zombie Action Plans. Doug scrambled from the floor and ran down the hallway, past the kitchen where the pot of water was boiling uncontrollably, through the lounge room and out onto the balcony.

He threw himself at the railing and froze. He'd always thought he could do this; a dramatic leap from the balcony, into the not-too-hard-looking tree, then shimmy to the ground. But now that the moment was here, he wasn't sure if even terror could override his sense of self-preservation.

He glanced over his shoulder. The creepy man was staring at him from beyond the windows. He wasn't making a move towards him—not yet—but the visage of him melting through the front door still burnt brightly in Doug's mind.

"Oh, hell," he moaned, and jumped.

The scream that escaped him as he fell wasn't nearly as masculine as he'd always imagined it would be, and it was cut short by the branches smashing into his chest. But Doug was impressed with himself by the way he clung to the tree and regained his equilibrium for a moment before dropping to the ground. Scrapes and possible bruises notwithstanding, Doug pulled himself up from the dirt and turned to run.

And collided with the barrelled chest of Capricorn.

He hit the ground for the third time in as many minutes and his blood turned to ice. This was it. He was going to die.

At least it wasn't in some boring, mundane, way.

"What the—!" he stammered. "How did you— *What* are you—!"

"I am not going to hurt you," the man told him. "We need to talk. And if Aquarius won't listen, then I guess it'll have to be with you." He reached down with one hand and wrenched Doug to his feet. Capricorn's eyes searched the surrounding low-rises as if expecting spies. "We'll talk inside," Capricorn said. "I'm not confident we're alone."

Doug trembled, staring up at this strange man with widened eyes. What was he? A demon? A witch? *Dude! You've been playing too many video games!* his mind screamed at him. *You know that stuff's not real!*

But how cool would it be if it was?

This was better than *End of Fantasy*. Like a real-life graphic novel, not under his fingertips, but standing in front of him. Standing—what was the word he'd used? *Incarnate.*

Of course, there was always the possibility that Doug was completely screwed.

"Okay," he said, though it was more like a whimper. "Err . . ." he faltered. "Can I offer you a drink?"

Doug was still shaking as he entered the lounge room, a glass of water in each hand, threatening to spill. The ghost of a smile appeared on Capricorn's lips, before he turned his head away.

Doug set the glasses on the coffee table and attempted a threatening glare. "What?"

"Nothing," Capricorn replied. "Just," he indicated the glasses on the table. "Water-bearer."

"Oh, har-har. Aquarius. I get it," Doug glowered. "Hate to ruin the mood, man. But I'm a Pisces."

Capricorn almost laughed. "How fitting," he said. "The incarnation of the new Age in the wrapping of the old." He bowed and shook his head, his smirk briefly deepening, before turning back to Doug. "You are not *an* Aquarius," he said mildly. "You are *the* Aquarius. The incarnation and embodiment of a fundamental spiritual force. As am I; I am Capricorn. The only difference is that you have somehow seen fit to remain Douglas Day, whereas I shed my human façade long ago. But the Dawning is upon us, and we need you to incarnate. Without you, this will all be for naught." "I've seen this anime, and it doesn't end well," Doug said.

"Pardon?"

"Never mind."

The loop of the starting menu for *End of Fantasy* began to play again for the umpteenth time. This was almost too much to take in. And yet, hadn't his love of comics and video games created fertile ground? Ground fertile enough to not only accept Capricorn's words, but *desire* them. His eyes turned briefly to the starting menu. Foreboding gave way to curiosity. "Hey, how did you walk through the wall?"

"When you are incarnate this physical world is no longer a hindrance to you," Capricorn replied. "Food, drink, sleep, these things are meaningless. The body is self-sustaining, as it should be. You can manifest and unmanifest at will, you *choose* which physical objects affect you. I am only sitting here because I *will it to be so.* Your door was only a barrier for as long as I chose. 'Form' is little more than 'space', and, when you incarnate, you will realise that space does not matter. Only *time* matters."

"So, this . . . 'Incarnating', what is it? A level-up? A magical transformation?"

Capricorn shook his head. "I don't follow."

"How does it work?"

Capricorn hesitated. "You just . . . Remember who you really are . . ."

Doug stared at him. Capricorn stared back.

"R-i-ght . . ." he finally drawled. "And, how do I do that?"

Capricorn rubbed at his face. There was a lethargy seeping from him that made him seem older again. It turned the squaring of his shoulders into a slump, the intensity of his gaze into a melancholic stare. For a moment, he seemed less like a demigod with the clippings turned off and more like a tired old man. "To be honest," he started cautiously, "I don't remember how."

Doug gave him a flat stare. "Really?"

"It's been a very long time," he admitted.

"Who were you? I mean, before you 'remembered' to be Capricorn?"

The look that returned his question was back to its penetrating form. "I was no-one," he replied. "What you have to understand is that person did not exist. Douglas Day does not exist. You *are* Aquarius. Day is just the clothes that you wear. He is meaningless."

Realisation dawned, but it dawned on a bitterly cold morn. "Are you saying that I'll die?" Doug asked.

"No."

"But *I* wouldn't be here, anymore." Doug stood from the couch and retreated a step. "You just said I'm meaningless."

"That's not what I meant—"

"But it's what you *said!*" Doug yelled. "Look, I know I'm not much, but I've become kinda fond of myself over the years, and if it means I'm going to die, then I don't know if I *want* to incarnate, or manifest, or incarnafest or maninate!"

"Douglas," Capricorn said, his jaw clenching. "You *are* Aquarius."

"Well, maybe I don't want to be!"

Capricorn stood and towered over him, eyes alight with fury. *"You have to be!"*

The floor shook, causing Doug to stagger. A noise came from below them as if the earth itself was groaning. The television swayed and the glasses on the table rattled and bounced across the surface, spilling droplets of water and threatening to topple. An earthquake? Another one? There'd already been one this morning, he'd read about it in the news. Doug grasped the back of the couch, his heart racing, as he tried to remember what to do in case of an earthquake; it wasn't a skill he thought he'd ever need, not in this city. A voice rang out in his head. *Capricorn!*

The man's face twisted as if in pain. He bowed his head, every muscle in his neck and shoulders standing with effort, and the shaking subsided. Capricorn raised his head, his eyes burning darkly.

"You have to be Aquarius," he spat, each word enunciated with care and threat. "The Ages *must* follow their proper order. Each Age is coloured by the characteristics of their ruler; the Age of Aries was a time of conflict; the Cancerian Age one of nurture. The Ages guide and propel the human race through their technological and spiritual growth, each building on the last. If the correct order is not followed then this—" he threw his hand towards the window "—*all of this,* will perish." Capricorn stepped closer, and Doug fought the urge to draw away. "The next Age is that of Aquarius. *Must be* that of Aquarius. For that, we need you to incarnate. We need you to *fight!*"

Doug stared at him, met the eyes lit with ferocious light. "Did you cause that earthquake?" he asked, his voice but a breath.

"Yes."

"And the one this morning?"

Capricorn deflated. "Yes," he admitted.

"Okay, that's kinda cool," Doug said.

Capricorn released a frustrated breath and fell into the couch.

"I'd incarnate for cool stuff like that," Doug said. "Only, I'm not really fond of the idea of dying for it."

"You won't die," Capricorn told him, his voice weary. "This person you are, this person you have become, is merely the incarnation you have chosen. For whatever reason you decided these personality traits are the traits *you* want to express at this time. You *have always been Aquarius.* You only need to remember that."

"Oh," Doug intoned. He sank down onto the couch. "Why didn't you say that in the first place?"

"Douglas," Capricorn said, and his tone was pleading. "It is not too light a statement to say that the fate of humankind is in your hands. But this coming Age, as with all things, is a *choice.* Everything we Twelve have built—everything we have been working toward for more than twenty millennia—hinges on the decision you make here. Now. Today." His face was drawn, muscles tight with uncertainty. "Please don't tell me I have wasted all that time."

The screen of the television had dimmed from inactivity, preparing to turn off. But still the starting menu of *End of Fantasy* was cycling. The subdued sound swelled to a crescendo, before it was suddenly cut off and the screen went black.

"Okay," Doug said—and there was a part of him, quite a large part, that couldn't believe he was saying the words. "I'll do it," he said.

He met Capricorn's questioning eyes.

"I'll help you save the world."

To be continued in the next edition of the Zodiac Series . . .

About the Author:

Helena McAuley won the Book Week prize in grade prep, and has been writing ever since—even though her spelling has not improved.

Lover of whisky, social justice, and adjectives, McAuley takes heart in the knowledge that reading activates the same brain centres as memory, and through reading Specific, we can remember every possible pasts, presents, and futures.

This is the Dawning is a serialised debut that will be published throughout the ASF Zodiac Series. So if you're wondering if Doug is up to the challenge of saving the world, you'll have to read Pisces (sorry/not sorry).

She can be found twit-ing, insta-ing, and occasionally facebooked under the handle @thathmc

Note: Unless you are the actual Aquarius, bearing water can be a sign of renal problems. Please consult your local GP.

ABOUT AUSSIE SPECULATIVE FICTION

Aussie Speculative Fiction is a recently established group which was created to support and promote Australian speculative fiction writers.

Check out our links:

www.facebook.com/Aussiespeculativefiction/

www.twitter.com/aussiefiction

www.aussiespeculativefiction.com

www.books2read.com/rl/asf

ABOUT DEADSET PRESS

Deadset Press is the publishing imprint of Aussie Speculative Fiction—a community aimed at supporting Australian and Kiwi authors. You can learn more at:

www.aussiespeculativefiction.com

ALSO BY DEADSET PRESS

Annual Anthologies

Beginnings: Aussie Speculative Fiction Anthology Vol.

Journeys: Aussie Speculative Fiction Anthology Vol. 2

Drowned Earth

Prequel: Shards of Silver by Alanah Andrews

The Rise by Sue-Ellen Pashley

Fire Over Troubled Water by Nick Marone

Submerged City by Austin P. Sheehan

Tides of War by Marcus Turner

The Jindabyne Secret by Jo Hart

River of Diamonds by S. M. Isaac

Salvaged by C.A. Clark

Emoto's Promise by Shel Calopa

<u>The Zodiac Series</u>

Capricorn (The Zodiac Series #1)

Aquarius (The Zodiac Series #2)

Pisces (The Zodiac Series #3)

Aries (The Zodiac Series #4)

Taurus (The Zodiac Series #5)

Gemini (The Zodiac Series #6)

Cancer (The Zodiac Series #7)

Leo (The Zodiac Series #8)

Virgo (The Zodiac Series #9)

Libra (The Zodiac Series #10)

Scorpio (The Zodiac Series #11)

Sagittarius (The Zodiac Series #12)